Brett walked around the room and didn't see anything strange. It was just an empty, dusty place that needed serious maid service.

He was about to leave when his eyes caught something shining on the floor. Kneeling down, he attempted to get a better look.

A few strands of reddish-brown hair were glinting against the sunlight, but the strange thing was that the pieces of hair were standing mostly upright, and appeared to disappear into a thin space between the wooden slats.

Without thinking, Brett reached down and pulled on the strands. But instead of giving away easily, more hair came through the space. He pulled on the hair, expecting it to eventually stop, when something thumped against the wood.

Holy shit. There's something connected to that hair.

A head? A person?

SUNKEN PARK

BY SARA BROOKE

The unrelenting heat of the Georgia sun was like a beacon of light leading tired motorists to the small ice cream shop that sat along the Pine Mountain highway.

The eatery was called The Purple Scoop and served the highest-caloric ice cream a person could possibly consume. In fact, most people who went in—left the eatery at least one pound heavier.

Frieda Parson, a stout, puffy sort of woman was intently focused on her milkshake and had propped herself up alongside her car while her husband Larry used the restroom inside. She was so busy sucking down the creamy concoction that she forgot that Larry had left the back door open. As the cookie dough bites traveled down her throat, her eyes never caught sight of her beagle, Buster, as he wriggled out of the backseat, hopped onto the road, and took off in the other direction. In fact, Frieda didn't notice that her dog was gone until she'd polished off the entire cup and went looking for a tissue to wipe off her sticky face.

While his owner was ravaging her dessert, Buster quickly wandered away from The Purple Scoop and after a three-mile trek that involved numerous territory markings, the little creature found himself at the entranceway of a park.

The beagle sniffed the air and whined for a minute. Something unseen caused him to sneeze and back up.

Something is bad here.

A sparrow flew out of the woods and landed on the closed gate that separated the park from Buster's tiny paws. A few seconds later, it flew up in the air and past Buster's head in a teasing manner.

The dog barked in excitement and spread his legs apart, ready for a chase.

The sparrow flew back over Buster's head and then took off toward the woods.

This time, the beagle didn't hesitate and chased after the bird, easily fitting underneath the gate and moving as quickly as his paws would allow. He raced past the trees and kept the bird within his view as it flew low to the ground and wove through the pine trees.

This continued for several minutes when suddenly, the sparrow flew up and disappeared amongst the branches.

Buster stopped for a moment and looked around. He was surrounded by greenery, but something about the scent made him wary of marking his territory.

The sound of crackling wood pierced the air and caused the dog to turn and seek out the intruder.

Buster didn't see anything strange, but sensed that something or someone was nearby. A deep growl emerged from his throat as the sunlight grew dimmer and shadows stretched out along the grass.

The darkness came quickly and wrapped itself around the air with a cold, ancient intensity. And in the distance, a figure moved toward the canine. It was hunched over and very old, but that didn't slow its pace.

Buster backed up, but there was nowhere to run, because he was now surrounded by a darkness that his innocent eyes had never experienced before. The dog yelped once and then went silent.

A moment later, the sparrow flew back through the trees and barely glanced at the collar that was now lying in the grass, glinting as the sunlight struck its polished surface.

CHAPTER 1

"They serve the absolute best breakfast here!"

Brett Duntman smiled as the blonde to his right devoured her scrambled eggs. He always liked women who were comfortable eating like a normal human being in front of a guy. And the beautiful Carrie Windler didn't mind scarfing down her breakfast like a true champion.

Carrie was smoking hot—one of the most attractive girls he'd seen in a long time. Despite going to college with some amazing-looking women, he'd been working on this particular beauty for quite a while. It had taken numerous walks along campus, phone calls about the lectures, and a few movie dates, but now she was his for an entire week.

"Dude, you gonna eat that?"

Brett's good friend and partner-in-crime Roy Johnson leaned over and snatched a piece of bacon off of his plate.

"Love me some bacon. Thanks for that," Roy said with a smile on his face.

Brett would have preferred to have Carrie all to himself, but she'd been hesitant to accompany him on the road trip until he had shared that there would be another couple joining them. He wasn't sure if she was really into him or if she was just looking for a fun weekend. Rumor had it that she was nursing a broken heart over a bad breakup, but he wasn't sure. Either way, she was *fine*, and he fully intended to have lots of sex before the weekend was over.

"That was totally delish," Carrie said, putting her fork on the plate. She smiled over at Brett and leaned back against the plush seat. "So what are we doing today?"

Brett wasn't sure. They'd been driving since five o'clock in the morning, eager to get on the road. But despite hoping to "bump" into some cool places, the highway had stretched long and winding before them, offering little in the way of recreation. The goal was to find a place on Pine Mountain to settle in for the night.

"There's a ton of places around here," said Roy's girlfriend, Anita Davila. Originally from Georgia, she had spent many summers vacationing in Callaway Gardens with her family. Memories of small, out-of-the-way parks and watering holes often flashed through her mind. Those were good times, and she held on to the happiness of the past. Since her mother's death a year prior, good thoughts had been few and far between. Though she never admitted it to Roy, she was really hoping that their mini vacation would help in the healing process.

Brett noticed Anita's wistful gaze and turned his eyes away, focusing on his breakfast.

When they all finished polishing off their food, Brett took the bill from the waitress and headed toward the cashier.

"That'll be thirty-five dollars, sir," said the attendant at the cash register in a cheerful Southern drawl.

Brett counted out the money and handed it to the woman. As he waited for change, his eyes were drawn to a display that was full of colorful brochures. Designed specifically for tourists, there were all sorts of photographs highlighting people in canoes, zip lining, and trekking through massive green forests.

The other members of his group also migrated over to the rack and started sifting through the different booklets.

"This stuff is so lame," said Roy as he flipped through a brochure. "Everything is so fucking expensive."

"And boring," Carrie added, laughing. "I mean, nature is great and everything, but I have no interest in walking through gardens in this heat."

"Or spending the day eating," Anita joined in. "Honestly, I don't like pecans or pies, or anything that makes me fat. Do you guys see anything else?"

Roy shook his head and turned to leave when he caught sight of a brochure that was tucked away in the back of the overstuffed rack. It was situated behind a series of brochures about an arts and crafts shop and was angled strangely; as if someone had pulled it out and then quickly shoved it back in.

"Yo, what's this?" Roy asked, pulling out the brochure and staring at it closely.

The words "Sunken Park" were emblazoned across the front of the brochure in big green letters. Each word was formed in the shape of intertwining vines, and the effect was ethereal. The brochure described the park as a local favorite and featured photos of people canoeing, grilling burgers, and gathered around a couch inside a cabin.

Roy started reading, "Enjoy the comforts that Pine Mountain, Georgia has to offer. Nestled deep within the mountain, Sunken Park is the perfect retreat to get away from the stress of life. The wonders of nature await you as you lose yourself in one of our many walking trails."

"If you enjoy spending time in the water, our mini-lakes provide the perfect respite from the heat. Float along in one of our canoes and take as much time as you want. Once a visitor rents a canoe, there is no time limit. You can float to your heart's content, all day long.

For those guests who want to spend the night in Sunken Park, there are large, resort-style cabins available that are clean and hospitable. Electricity and running water are readily available while you sleep to the sounds of crickets."

Roy stopped for a minute and then flipped to the back of the brochure. "Holy shit! You only have to pay ten bucks for parking and the rest of it is free." He looked up and smiled at Brett. "We should totally do this, dude. Come on. You can't get any better than this."

Brett took the brochure from his friend and examined it carefully. The park wasn't located that far from where they were, but something about the idea had him feeling slightly uneasy.

The brochure itself was professionally designed, but the actual paper it was printed on seemed worn. The edges were frayed and the fold felt flimsy, as if it would tear at any moment.

Brett frowned and was about to question whether or not

they should just keep looking when Carrie put her hand on his shoulder.

"I think that sounds like a great idea," she said happily. "For ten dollars we have a place to stay? You really can't beat that kind of deal. I'm in."

Anita smiled and nodded in agreement.

Brett felt like the odd man out and was about to suggest that they ask the cashier about the park when Roy snatched the brochure out of his hand and headed outside. There was nothing left to do but follow the group out of the restaurant and into the sweltering heat.

To pass the time, Anita suggested they listen to an audio book.

Everyone in the car groaned, but she was determined, and within a few minutes a flat voice flowed through the speakers, putting both Carrie and Roy to sleep.

While Carrie snored gently in the passenger's seat, Brett drove along the highway, trying to relax. He knew that the idea of spending time alone with Carrie was making him nervous, but it was something else too.

Ten bucks? Seems too good to be true.

Normally a slightly skeptical person, Brett wasn't sure if they would find what they were looking for at Sunken Park. He knew from experience that you usually got what you paid for, but he wasn't exactly swimming in cash and the idea of getting a bunch of recreational enjoyment for virtually nothing was very appealing.

Sighing, he looked around the car at all the sleeping faces. Anita was now nodding off as well, her head resting against the glass and vibrating as the tires stumbled over worn pavement and loose gravel.

When he turned his gaze back to the windshield, he tried to focus on the road and the scenery that just seemed to stretch on and on.

Trees and large boulders hugged the highway as his car began the winding ascent up the mountain. Every once in a while, the GPS woman would remind him of the direction in her clipped, cold voice. A cooler in the trunk shifted back and forth on each turn, stuffed tightly with snacks and drinks from a quick stop at a mini-mart along the way. The brochure had clearly indicated that alcohol was not allowed on the premises, but that didn't stop the group from picking up a six-pack and a bottle of wine.

The car began traveling along a stretch of road that was steeper now, and the contents of the car began to sharply shift back and forth as Brett navigated up the winding semicircles.

"Sunken Road approaching in one-point-five miles. On right."

Brett squinted to see if any roads were clearly visible to his right, but all he could see was dense foliage packed together. He tried to slow down, but it was too late and the small road sign he'd been looking for seemed to pop up out of nowhere, causing him to slam on the brakes.

Everyone shrieked as the car lurched forward and after sliding a few inches—finally stopped moving, its tires skidding along the gravel that lined the highway.

Brett quickly looked in the rearview mirror and was relieved when he saw that no one was behind him. He quickly put the car in reverse and turned down Sunken Road, which was nothing more than a medium-sized stretch of dirt.

"Dude," Roy complained, rubbing the back of his neck. "Could you please give us a little warning next time? That wasn't cool. You nearly broke my neck."

"I'm sorry," Brett apologized. "These roads are really tough to navigate up here, and I don't remember the map indicating that this is a dirt road. I'm surprised my GPS even found it."

Carrie and Anita were silent and watched as the car navigated through the trees. Huge pines surrounded them on all sides like silent sentries of the forest. Along each side of the road, the ground seemed to drop several feet, and jutted out in random spots with miniature ledges that were covered with moss and dirt.

The feeling of being completely surrounded was slightly suffocating. Brett recalled passing an ice cream shop a few miles back, but that was the last form of civilization they'd seen. He considered turning the car around when they passed a white sign with "Sunken Park 1 mile" painted on it.

"Hey, at least they've got a sign," Carrie said, trying to lighten the mood. "I can't wait to get out of this car and stretch out a bit."

Brett appreciated her comment and reached over to squeeze her leg. Her skin felt wonderful, and he could almost forget about the strange woods they were traveling through.

Almost.

The car traveled slowly through the woods, until the trees began to spread out and finally, opened up to a grassy knoll. At the far end of the clearing sat a large metal gate with a sign stating "Sunken Park" affixed to one of the arms. The gate, however, was closed, making it impossible to pass through to the park on the other side.

Brett pulled the car up to the gate and put it into park.

"I'm going to see what's going on. Just wait here for a minute."

The group murmured in agreement.

Brett stepped out of the idling vehicle and looked at the gate. It didn't seem to be locked, and he could see a small building a few feet back. It was painted white and green, and he figured that it was some sort of headquarters for the people who ran the park.

As he approached the closed gate, the door to the office opened and a person stepped out.

Brett squinted against the sunlight that was now shining freely, unobstructed by the surrounding trees. He could barely make out the figure walking toward him, but as the person approached he could see that it was a man in his fifties or sixties.

As the man came to the edge of the gate, Brett could now make out his features. He figured the man was a park ranger by the telltale khaki clothing he wore and the large-brimmed hat on his head. The man's skin was brown and leathery—a sign of many hours spent under the glaring sun.

Brett decided to introduce himself right away, though he wasn't sure if the park was open since the closed gates weren't exactly welcoming them in.

"Hi, my name's Brett Duntman. We'd like to visit the park. Are you open?"

The ranger was quiet for a moment and then broke out into a grin. Yellowed teeth appeared from behind cracked lips. "Sure thing. Sorry about the gates. Name's Jack Blaze. I'm in charge of the park for the weekend. Give me a minute and I'll open these up for ya."

Brett nodded and headed back to the car. Once he was inside, the cool flow of air conditioning felt wonderful against his face. Even though he'd only been outside for a few minutes, the heat and humidity had been nearly unbearable..

"So what's the deal?" asked Anita. "I see that guy unlocking the gates. Is the park open?"

"Yep. It looks like we're in luck," Brett replied, pulling the car past the gates and up to the building.

Jack was standing outside waiting for them and tipped his hat when they all got out of the car. "Nice meeting you folks. You've come to visit us here on a beautiful day. Should be a great one."

Anita, Roy, and Carrie smiled politely as they stretched their legs and looked around.

The park was vast, with pine trees covering the landscape for as far as they could see. The terrain was hilly and in the distance a medium-sized body of water glistened against the sunlight. Anita could see at least one cabin in the distance, nestled against the trees like a snug child under warm covers.

"This place is beautiful," she breathed.

Roy smiled and came over to his girlfriend, putting his arm around her shoulders.

"This is just what we needed," he whispered in her ear.

She smiled and kissed him gently on the mouth, pulling his large body close to hers.

After Brett paid for parking, Jack requested that the group sit down on a park bench so that he could go over "the rules."

"We're pretty slow this weekend," Jack started. "There's a big weekend-long eco-tour going on in Atlanta and that's got most people's attention. So, aside from a few other stragglers, you've got most of the park to yourselves."

"That's great!" said Roy. "So can we take any cabin we want?"

Jack grinned and continued, "Unfortunately, because we knew it would be slow, we're performing some maintenance on most of the cabins. But we do have one available and it's clearly marked on the map I'm going to give ya and pretty easy to find. You'll be staying in Cabin C and it's a short walk from here, so you should be able to carry your personal items over there."

"Wait," interrupted Brett. "You mean no one's going to escort us over there? We have to find our own way?"

"Dude, don't be such a chicken shit," Roy joked. "That's totally normal for camping. We'll find it just fine. Don't worry, ladies. I'll be the keeper of the map and your guide for the afternoon." He knelt down on one knee and winked at Carrie and Anita, causing them to break out into giggles.

"Actually," Jack said a bit more sternly than before, "you probably shouldn't be wandering around in the woods at night. During the day it's fine and you should be able to find your way pretty easily. But at night we advise our guests to stay close to their cabins because the woods can get pretty dark, and it's easy to get lost."

The group was silent as Jack's words sank in. They hadn't been expecting to explore the woods at night, but hearing the warning was a sharp reminder of the fact that they were surrounded by nature and far from the amenities and protection they were used to.

"No problem," Brett said, trying to reassure the park ranger. "We'll follow all of your rules. We're just here to catch some rest and relaxation."

Jack didn't immediately respond and went back inside the building.

"Where's he going?" Anita asked.

"I've got no idea, but that guy needs to get out more," Roy joked.

A minute later, Jack appeared holding two maps in his hand. "Now, folks, here's a couple of maps of the property. It's pretty easy to follow and all I ask is that you mind the rules and keep your cabin clean so that other people can enjoy it after you're gone. Have fun."

The man turned to leave when suddenly Carrie blurted out a question. "Why is this place called Sunken Park?"

The question seemed to have come out of nowhere, but Jack didn't appear surprised.

"Well, miss, let's just say that the park is built on soil that tends to get soft when it rains. So don't stand still for too long in any one spot. Have a good day."

And with that, the park ranger flashed a strange grin, tipped his hat, and went back inside the office.

CHAPTER 2

Despite Jack's assurance that Cabin C was only a short walk, the heat and humidity made the trek difficult. Brett could feel sweat traveling down his forehead and along the sides of his face as he struggled with the bags.

Carrie had complained a few yards back that she was exhausted, so Brett had agreed to lug some of her stuff, as well. And women never packed light, so her bags felt like sacks of sand. Still, he didn't want to seem weak, so he continued along quietly.

As they walked deeper into the park, the beauty of Mother Nature greeted them at every corner. Pine trees swayed in the occasional breeze and the smell of fresh grass was intoxicating.

The only strange thing about the park was the absence of other visitors. Carrie noticed the silence of their surroundings, only interrupted by the compression of leaves under their sneakers.

"It's so quiet here," she remarked, looking around at the vast woods.

"Yeah," agreed Anita. "But you know, I think it's actually kind of cool. Hey, look, there's one of the other cabins!"

The group stopped for a moment and looked back.

In the distance, the reddened logs of a cabin peeked out from within a mass of trees and bushes. It appeared vacant, but for just a minute Anita thought she saw a dark shape appear by one of the windows.

She stopped and squinted, trying to get a better look, but Roy was tugging at her arm insistently.

"Let's go. These bags weigh a ton!"

Anita could no longer see anything in or near the cabin and turned back to face her impatient boyfriend, giving him her sweetest gaze.

"Stop rushing me. I'm coming."

Carrie thought her feet were literally going to dissolve beneath her ankles by the time their cabin finally came into view.

"We're here!" she announced.

The cabin itself looked unimpressive and small, the logs a dull brown and a thin film of spider webs extending out and wrapping itself around the different corners of the structure. A dirt path started at the front door and extended out into the woods.

Pine trees surrounded the small structure, their branches hanging overhead and providing a welcoming shroud of shade. A small fire pit had been built close by and was contained by a set of medium-sized boulders. A pile of loose ash inside the pit indicated that at one time there'd been other guests enjoying the warmth of a fire during a cool night.

Brett went up to the door and tugged on the knob. They hadn't been given keys to the cabin, but Jack had assured them that they were in such a remote place that theft was unheard of, and it was safe to leave their belongings unattended.

As he pushed the door open, the interior slowly came into view.

"Wow, this is really nice," Anita said, surprised by the hospitable furnishings given how rudimentary their cabin had appeared from the outside.

The group slowly made its way inside, amazed at how furnished and resort-like the cabin actually was.

The floors were clean and bright. A set of leather couches rested near a fireplace and were adorned by colorful blankets.

The kitchen appeared nearly brand new, with silver-colored appliances and granite countertops. Little knickknacks were scattered throughout, giving the appearance of a country kitchen.

The two bedrooms were a furnished with large beds, flat-screen TVs, and had adjoining bathrooms that were clean and modern.

The couples stepped inside and quickly chose their rooms. After setting their bags down on the beds, they reconvened back in the kitchen.

"Shit, my cell phone doesn't work out here," Anita complained. "How am I going to survive without the internet for a weekend? I need to check my emails!"

Roy, Carrie, and Brett checked their phones as well and had the same result.

No service.

"Well, at least we're going to be able to disconnect from the world. This is really nice. I think we're going to have a great time here," Roy said, lifting the cooler and placing it on the counter. "I'd like to check out one of those hiking trails before we eat some lunch. Anita, do you want to come with me?"

Anita looked over at Carrie, who was busy putting the beers and food into the refrigerator. She didn't want to leave her with all the work, but it seemed like most of the food was getting put away and she could tell from the look in Roy's eyes that he was hoping for a little "private time."

"Carrie, is it ok if I take off for a bit? Do you need help with anything else?"

Carrie smiled as she lifted the wine out of the cooler. "No problem. I'm almost done here anyway. Go out and enjoy. We'll be fine."

Anita smiled and grabbed Roy's hand as the two left the cabin.

Brett watched as Anita and Roy disappeared among the trees. His heart began to race at the realization that he was now alone with Carrie for the first time since they'd left the college campus.

She was washing a glass in the kitchen, but turned up to look at him and smiled.

Not waiting for a special invitation, Brett walked up and took the glass out of her hand. He stared into her eyes and instinctively brushed a few strands of hair away from her forehead. His body was alive and aroused, and there was no turning back.

Leaning forward, he kissed her lips with passion and

purpose, feeling her body succumb to him. Her tongue emerged from soft lips and found his, bringing him waves of pure desire.

They kissed and moaned as their bodies moved closer and finally began to rub gently back and forth.

Brett led Carrie out of the kitchen and into the bedroom, where he laid her down and removed her clothes. Within minutes, they were both naked and writhing on the bed, their passions hot and hungry.

Outside, the trees gently swayed in unison as the couple made love.

But something else was watching them …

… and waiting.

CHAPTER 3

Anita wasn't fond of the water.

For starters, she wasn't a great swimmer. But she was able to manage in a regular pool.

This, however, was a lake that was full of fish and gunk and lord knows what else.

After walking for about ten minutes, they'd come upon the outskirts of one of the park's mini-lakes. Roy had immediately stripped off his clothes and taken a dive into the dark depths completely naked.

Anita, on the other hand, wasn't sure she wanted to join him.

"Come on, babe," Roy called out, trying to coax her into the water.

"No, that's ok. I'll sit here and watch you."

Anita found a rotting log and quickly sat down, happy to relax after trekking through the woods in the overbearing heat. But as her body quickly lowered itself onto the wood, she felt something sharp tear at the back of her left leg.

"Ouch!" she yelled, and twisted her body around, trying to get a closer look at the source of the pain.

"You ok?" Roy called out.

"Yeah, yeah," Anita responded, turning her leg so that she could see the back of it. A thin trickle of blood was traveling down her skin in a slim red line. She knelt down to see the portion of the wood that had cut into her and immediately saw a piece that was jutting out.

The wood looked old, and there were white spots dotting the brown crusty surface.

Anita felt a lump in her throat at the sight of the rotting spike.

Dear God. I hope I didn't get any bugs or bacteria on me.

She pulled a tissue out of her pocket and wiped off the blood as best as she could. Then she walked over to the water's edge to wait for her boyfriend.

The water was cold, but it felt wonderful against Roy's skin. He ducked his head underneath the cool waves and enjoyed the feel of the liquid against his sweaty face.

When he emerged, he could see Anita standing on the banks waiting for him, but he had already drifted farther out. He waved and shouted, "I'll be a few more minutes!"

Anita nodded, but he could tell she was pissed.

She was always pissed off these days. It didn't take much to upset her now that her mother was gone. It was difficult for him to deal with.

Roy was a happy-go-lucky kind of person and had been attracted to Anita when he'd met her two years prior because she'd been the same way. But then the cancer had arrived and ravaged her poor mother within a matter of months, the happiness he'd grown to love had been extinguished and replaced by moodiness and depression.

She'd been seeing a therapist to deal with her emotions, but the trauma had taken a toll on their relationship.

In the beginning, Anita had been extremely sexual and wanted to make love on a regular basis. For Roy, this was a refreshing change from other women who always wanted to wait to have sex, and then, when it finally happened, expected professions of love to come shortly after orgasm. With Anita, there hadn't been any issues with sex before love. She was comfortable with her body, and they'd spent hours exploring each other underneath sweaty sheets in her dorm room.

But after her mother's death, things changed.

When she was in one of her "moods," Anita didn't want him to touch her. She never seemed to climax during sex anymore, either. And when they were intimate, he sometimes felt like she was far away—locked in a nightmare of her own making. It was frustrating to feel so distant from the woman he loved.

He was hoping this trip would change all of that.

Roy.

The voice was so soft that he almost didn't hear it. He looked around, searching for the source, but there was nothing there—just more water and the other side of the lake.

Roy.

This time Roy didn't only hear his name being whispered, but he also felt a cool breeze against his face. It almost felt like the wind was passing through him, and he began to feel numbness throughout his body. It crept through his skin as he treaded water and crept along until he could actually feel a haziness enter his mind. The sensation wasn't unpleasant, just strange and calming.

Without thinking about it, he repositioned his body and began floating on his back. As his ears connected with the water, he felt sleepy and strange.

Roy … the woods … we are waiting here for you … the woods …

The voice was now emanating from the depths of the water and Roy could almost sense the vowels as they bubbled up from a gentle, safe place. He closed his eyes as the voice began to carry him along the waves, and his mind threatened to completely cloud over.

"Roy! Roy!"

The sound of Anita's panicked voice cut through the water like knives piercing through a pillow. Roy lost his balance and thrashed in the water for a moment, choking as some of the murky liquid poured into his windpipe.

Sputtering, he rose to the surface and could see that Anita was incredibly pissed and standing right at the waterline.

"What, honey?" he called out, trying to keep the irritation out of his voice. He still felt very weird, but figured it had something to do with all the heat they were in.

"I'm tired of standing here, that's what," she called out. "Can we please go back to the cabin? I cut myself and want to put a bandage on it."

"Sure thing. I'm coming."

Roy began to swim to the shore, but he wondered if the

voice would call out to him again.

The waters were now silent, and he was almost disappointed that the strange, hypnotic voice had disappeared. Whatever it had been, it hadn't been unpleasant, and he preferred that calming sensation to the stress his girlfriend was no doubt about to unleash upon him.

He kicked harder and finally made it to the shore—just in time to get scolded by Anita for taking too long in the water.

"Ouch, it really hurts!" Anita whined as Carrie applied some hydrogen peroxide to the cut on her leg. When she and Roy had returned to the cabin, both Carrie and Brett had appeared a bit disheveled and sweaty. It was quite obvious that they'd been having sex.

Anita wasn't sure if she was ready to increase the frequency of her lovemaking sessions with Roy. She knew he was a sexual person with strong needs, and he was constantly kissing her in an attempt to strengthen their intimacy. But she was still mourning the loss of her mother and felt alone most of the time. The constant feeling of singularity and vulnerability made it very difficult for her to let go of the binds that held tightly. And it made for absolutely terrible sex.

To top it off, the cut on her leg was hurting like a motherfucker and she hoped it wasn't infected. Carrie had been great and instantly descended upon her with a Band-Aid and antiseptic.

But when Carrie had applied the hydrogen peroxide the solution had bubbled up instantly, possibly indicating that bacteria had found its way into the cut, which wasn't a good thing. Ever since her mother's death, Anita had become a nervous hypochondriac and worried about every little cut and bruise. Illness wasn't something she was comfortable dealing with.

"It's going to be fine," Carrie assured her. "It's just a cut, and even though it's a little swollen, I'm sure it will start scabbing over by tomorrow morning. Just leave it alone and let the antiseptic work its magic."

Anita smiled at the attractive blonde. Initially she had been wary of Carrie because of the whole "sorority girl/ cheerleader" type thing, but she was discovering that the woman was actually a kind-hearted person who was friendly and helpful.

"Thanks," she said smiling.

"No prob. Now, let's grab these sandwiches and go eat!"

The group gathered up the array of sandwiches and chips that Brett and Carrie had set on the counter and carried everything out to the porch, where the sun was already beginning its descent in the west.

"I can't believe the day has passed so quickly," Brett said, looking at his watch. "It's five o'clock already, and we're just now eating lunch."

"Well, someone was a little busy," Roy teased, giving Carrie a knowing glance. "Y'all probably worked up a little bit of an appetite."

Carrie blushed and looked away, focusing on her sandwich.

"What were you guys up to? When you got back you looked like you'd just taken a shower," Brett remarked, trying to change the subject.

"I took a quick jump in the pond or the lake or whatever the hell it is," Roy answered as he munched on his chips. "But Anita chickened out, so she had the pleasure of watching me float along."

"Yeah," Anita grumbled. "I got a chance to stand there with my bleeding leg while you enjoyed the water. And you were so caught up in your own little world that you didn't even hear me calling you to come back in."

"Next time you'll have to join me," Roy responded lightly, and then gave his girlfriend a big smile to ease some of the tension.

Anita shifted painfully and then jumped up. Her plate fell off of her lap and a half-eaten sandwich as well as a full bag of chips tumbled to the ground.

"Ouch!" She cried. "That damned cut really hurts. I think I'm going to go inside and watch a movie on my laptop."

The outburst was completely unexpected, and no one was exactly sure what to say. Silence hung in the air for a few seconds, when Carrie finally stood up and took control of the situation.

"That's fine. I'll sit with you. I'm tired anyway. Let's pick up this food and then go relax."

The women quickly cleaned up the mess and went inside together, leaving the men alone on the porch.

"Damn," Roy sighed. "She is just so fucking emotional all the time. It's annoying."

Brett wasn't sure what to say. He knew that the couple was having problems, but didn't want to put himself in the middle of it. When he interfered in other peoples' business, it never turned out well.

"Look, she's probably just tired and hot. I mean, we've been driving all day, and then she had to take a long walk and ended up getting cut, which is never fun. Just give her some girl time with Carrie. I'm sure she'll be fine."

But Roy wasn't convinced and began to feel uncomfortable and edgy. It occurred to him that it might be a good idea to wander through the woods and get away from all the drama.

"Hey, do you want to go for a walk in the woods? I mean, it's pretty cool out there. Why don't we look for those other cabins?"

Brett agreed. It was probably a good idea to give the girls some alone time.

He stood up and quickly went back to the front door, opening it and peering inside.

Carrie and Anita were already sitting on the couch next to each other, the laptop on the small coffee table in front of them, and some chick-flick music reverberating out of the tiny speakers. They looked content, though Anita's cheeks were a bit flushed, and for a moment Brett wondered if perhaps she might be coming down with something.

Nah, it's just a little scratch. She'll be fine.

"Ladies, we're going to take a little walk in the woods. We'll be back in a few minutes."

Carrie nodded and smiled.

Anita ignored him entirely.

Taking a deep breath, Brett closed the door and turned to join his friend, who had already stepped off the porch and was heading toward the woods.

After Brett and Roy left the cabin, Carrie felt the need to use the bathroom. She excused herself and let out a deep breath as she sat down on the toilet.

Damn, there is some serious stress between Anita and Roy. That relationship is in trouble.

Once she finished urinating, Carrie stood up and flushed. She then went over to the sink to wash her hands. But when she looked in the mirror to check her hair, she gasped and found herself staring into the face of a hag.

The only shared resemblance she had with the horrible-looking woman in the mirror was the fact that they both had pale skin. But that was where the similarity ended.

The hag had frizzy, reddish brown hair with folds of wrinkled skin hanging from her cheeks and chin. Her eyes were rheumy and dripping at the corners, and there was spittle leaking from the side of her mouth.

The hag grinned, revealing blackened teeth and a mouth that just kept getting larger and larger until it began to fill the creature's face.

Carrie screamed and felt her feet buckle as the floor rose to meet her in a gaping hole of merciful darkness.

CHAPTER 4

Brett was awed and slightly intimidated by the heavy foliage that surrounded them. Pine trees were everywhere, and the only thing that kept him and Roy from getting lost was a small dirt path that had been flattened into the ground to help visitors navigate through the shrubbery. Without the path, however, he knew it would be easy to get lost.

He shuddered at the thought. The idea of wandering around the vast woods in the dark was totally unappealing. The park ranger had warned them of the uneven terrain, and Brett could see that there were no lights to guide travelers in the event of a midnight trek.

Looks like all you'd have is the light of the moon. But I'll bet it sounds a helluva lot more romantic than it actually is. I think I'll stay indoors when the sun goes down.

"Hey, wait up!"

To Brett's frustration, Roy was moving ahead quite rapidly. It was a bit strange, because he wasn't talking much and just seemed to be wandering—albeit quickly—along the path.

Brett tried to strike up a conversation, hoping to pass the time and perhaps raise his friend's spirits. The argument with Anita had no doubt caused some stress and perhaps a bit of embarrassment.

"So whaddaya think of all this? You think we're gonna see some hot women in the other cabin? Might make for a fun night!" Brett laughed at his own joke, but Roy continued walking ahead.

"Roy, are you ok?"

There was no immediate response, but Roy stopped walking

and scratched his head absentmindedly.

"Yeah, sorry about that. Just seem to be in my own little world this afternoon. What were you saying?"

Brett didn't feel like repeating himself and he felt like his joke was stupid anyway, so he changed the subject.

"I think that cabin's up here somewhere. Hey, there it is!"

As Roy and Brett walked along the path, the cabin that the group had passed earlier slowly came into view. It looked shabby and old, and was surrounded by ugly overgrown weeds. A red "B" had been painted on the upper right-hand side near the door, but much of the paint had started chipping away. Its windows were a hazy shade of gray and cobwebs hung down droopily from every corner.

Brett recalled Jack's comment about the fact that many of cabins were undergoing necessary renovations, and now he could see why. Cabin B definitely needed fine-tuning. Curious as to whether or not someone was staying inside, he stepped up to the door and knocked slowly a few times.

No one answered, but to his surprise, the door moved slightly and he realized that it was ajar. Inky blackness seemed to seep out of the sliver of air that escaped through the opening.

"Do you think I should go in?"

"Yeah, sure," Roy answered. "I'll wait out here for you."

Brett didn't like the idea of going into the cabin by himself, and for a second he experienced pangs of fear that he quickly shook off.

Stop being such a pussy. I'm a grown man. There's nothing to be afraid of.

He reached out and pushed the door fully open, peering into the gloominess within.

Taking a deep breath, Brett stepped inside. As his eyes adjusted to the darkness, he found his surroundings dusty and depressing.

The cabin was furnished similarly to the cabin that the group was staying in, but everything looked very old and worn. In fact, some of the furniture seemed to be from another decade and resembled the décor that Brett's parents had purchased in the 1970s. He recalled photographs of his mother casually sprawled out on a couch that had long fabric resembling shag carpet and wallpaper in the kitchen that was covered in large prints.

He chuckled as he walked around the structure. The cabin clearly hadn't been a part of the park renovations yet and was just short of disgusting.

Not going to see any hotties here. Just a whole lotta nothing.

He sighed and turned to go when a sound caught his attention. He couldn't quite figure out what it was, but it sounded like someone was running their nails against the wooden floorboards.

His blood ran cold.

What the hell was that? The cabin's empty, isn't it? Maybe it's an animal.

Brett stood still for a minute, waiting to see if he'd hear any other sounds. He could feel all of his muscles tense up and small beads of sweat began to appear along his forehead.

Seconds ticked by as he waited, but no sound.

Then, just as he was about to turn and leave, he heard it again. It sounded like a thud, and he could actually feel the wooden floorboards vibrate slightly.

Roy better not be fucking around. This is scaring the shit outta me.

Brett looked over in the direction of one of the bedrooms and decided to invesigate. Carefully walking over to the closed door, he shakily placed his hand on the knob.

Scenes from a million horror movies flashed through his mind.

If something jumps out at me from the other side, I'm gonna lose my mind.

Taking another deep breath, Brett quickly pushed the door open and backed away.

The door swung open, connecting with the wall as its whiny hinges squealed in irritation. Jarred by the movement, dust traveled down from the frame and landed on the floor.

Brett cautiously stepped into the doorway and looked around.

The room was sparsely furnished with a small single bed and a wooden dresser of drawers. Dust had settled on everything and intermingled with the sunlight that was coming through a single cloudy window. A cockroach emerged from one end of the room and quickly scurried underneath the bed.

This place is nasty. Don't they ever clean?

Brett walked around the room and didn't see anything strange. It was just an empty, dusty place that needed serious maid service.

He was about to leave when his eyes caught something shining on the floor. Kneeling down, he attempted to get a better look.

A few strands of reddish-brown hair were glinting against the sunlight, but the strange thing was that the pieces of hair were standing mostly *upright*, and appeared to disappear into a thin space between the wooden slats.

Without thinking, Brett reached down and pulled on the strands. But instead of giving away easily, more hair came through the space. He pulled on the hair, expecting it to eventually stop, when something thumped against the wood.

Holy shit. There's something connected to that hair.

A head? A person?

A small gasp escaped Brett's lips as he dropped the hair he was holding and backed away. The strands fell gently to the ground and landed in a pile.

Brett could sense that something was wrong and wanted to run, but his feet weren't listening and he remained frozen in place. He watched the strands of hair for movement, but they remained still among the dust.

Outside, he could hear leaves crackling and realized that Roy was leaving.

He can't leave me here. Is he insane?

Suddenly, Brett thought he saw the hair moving, ever so slightly. It was all he needed to find the energy in his legs, and he turned and fled.

As he tore through the living room and ran for the door, he heard it again ...

... Thud.

As consciousness returned and she awakened from her unnatural sleep, dust floated up into Carrie's nostrils, making her sneeze. The act caused pain to shoot through her skull, causing her to sit up in agony.

"Oww! Damn, that hurts!" she exclaimed, putting a hand on her forehead. When she pulled it away she was relieved to find that there was no blood on her palm.

How the hell did I end up on the floor?

Gingerly standing up, Carrie noticed the mirror and the memory came back quickly.

The hag staring at her.

Gasping, Carrie backed up and looked away. She wasn't entirely sure what she'd seen in the mirror, but didn't want to take any chances. And the idea that she'd actually fainted was quite scary, because that wasn't something that normally happened.

Maybe it's just low blood sugar and I need to eat something else.

Carrie looked down at her watch and was surprised that a half hour had passed and it was nearly sundown. She opened the bathroom door and peered into the gloomy cabin. The laptop screen on the coffee table was dark, indicating the movie had ended.

But where was Anita?

"Anita, are you ok?" she called out. "I'm sorry I was in the bathroom for so long. I must have tripped and fallen on the floor, but I'm ok now."

There was no answer at first, but Carrie thought she heard a soft moan.

Concerned now, she walked toward the couch to see what was going on. As she neared the leather sofa, she noticed that it was covered in a light sheen of dust. It wasn't something they'd noticed before, and she wondered if maybe the dust was making them all a little sick.

A low moan emerged once more.

Walking to the front of the couch, Carrie knelt down and looked at Anita, who appeared to be asleep with her face turned towards the cushions.

"Anita, are you ok?" she asked again.

"No, I'm sick," Anita mumbled, but it was difficult to hear her because she was leaning her forehead against the leather cushions, and her face was resting closely against the material.

"Well, why don't we see what your temperature is?" Carrie suggested and gently turned the woman to face her.

As Anita turned, Carrie was stunned to discover that a few pieces of the woman's skin had remained on the leather cushions.

Oh my God. She's got some sort of flesh-eating virus.

Anita's face was red, and her skin was raw and bleeding. In some places the skin was peeling off entirely, revealing red, oozing patches of infection. Her eyes were wet and glazed over, and her breathing seemed labored.

Carrie was a pre-med major in college and had seen photographs of people with different types of illnesses including Ebola, malaria, and dysentery. Anita looked like she had a bacterial infection called necrotizing fasciitis, with the harsh and sometimes fatal symptoms well underway.

Carrie knew that when a person was diagnosed with having a flesh-eating bacterial infection there wasn't much time to waste and medical attention was an urgent necessity. But the guys were nowhere to be found, and she wasn't exactly going to trek through the woods with the sick woman, so she had no choice but to wait.

As she sat on the edge of the couch, Carrie continued to say calming words to Anita, but her mind was racing in other directions.

I shouldn't have gone on this vacation. Brett is nice and all, but I really should've waited longer to have sex with him. Guys always act weird after they have sex for the first time, and sometimes they just disappear altogether.

It was too soon after Greg.

We had such an amazing time together. Why did he get all cold and start blowing me off? It's not like I'm an ugly duckling. Ok, I know I wasn't all that attractive in junior high school or even high school, but I've kinda blossomed. So why do the guys I like the most still treat me like I'm nothing?

Maybe Brett isn't so bad. But this trip just feels like a mistake.

Mom always says you've got to go slow or guys won't respect you. And look, we just have sex and Brett takes off for—

"Carrie?" Anita's voice cut through the air and jarred Carrie back to reality.

"What, honey?" she asked gently.

"I feel like I'm going to throw up."

"Ok, let me help you to the bathroom. Let's take it slowly."

s she gently helped the woman to her feet, one thought formed in Carrie's mind.

Brett, please get back here soon.

Roy wished Brett would hurry up and come back outside. He wanted to keep walking and follow the siren sounds of nature that seemed to be calling to him again.

He'd felt it while they were still with the girls. It sounded like a low buzzing in his ears like a fly flitting too close to his eardrums. But it wasn't unpleasant or annoying like a real insect. It was a comforting sound that seemed to be guiding him through the woods.

The sound had stopped as they'd gotten closer to Cabin B, and Roy had a feeling that whatever it was, it wanted him to keep walking.

As he stood outside and listened for the buzzing, the wind gently picked up and rustled the trees that surrounded the small cabin. The wind sounded like it was gently moaning and reminded Roy of beautiful fall days back in Oregon.

As a child, fall had been his favorite season. He loved sitting outside while his dad raked the leaves and talked to him about different things. It had always felt like their special time together, with the crisp smell of cooling air around them. Sometimes they would wait for the perfect moment and then jump into a big pile of leaves, lying on their backs and staring at the sky.

Roy had always known that his father was a special man, and that not all parents were as attentive to their kids. In fact, many of his friends' parents were too busy working or doing "adult things" to spend time with their children. So he treasured these precious moments and remembered them fondly.

The weather outside, despite being in the middle of summer, had changed and the temperature dropped nearly twenty degrees. Roy was feeling so distant and hazy that a sudden change in temperature and condition didn't frighten him or seem odd. If anything, it was a welcome respite and an additional drug that continued to pull him further and further from reality.

Instead of waiting for Brett to emerge from the cabin, Roy felt his feet pulling him in another direction. He could sense the wind turning and blowing circles around him as if creating an invisible lasso that was gently pulling him deeper into the woods.

He allowed himself to be guided deeper and deeper into the surrounding nature. The trees were denser here and blocked out the sun. The temperature continued to drop and now Roy felt as if he truly was in the midst of fall. He could feel the wind continue to blow and push the tree branches in different directions. At times, leaves would tumble to the ground as he walked past. And still he continued on.

Roy began to smell smoke and wondered if someone was burning something. As he approached a clearing, he could see a group of people standing in the center of it. A bonfire had been built and small flames licked at the darkened logs, sending smoke into the air.

The people were deep in discussion and didn't seem to notice Roy as he approached. He decided to play it safe and hid behind the trees, straining to hear what they were saying. As he waited, the volume of their conversation started to rise.

It occurred to Roy that the sudden change in volume was similar to a person turning up the sound on a television or radio. He tried to ignore the strangeness of the moment—straining to hear what the people in the clearing were saying.

Theye were speaking with strong southern accents and seemed to be debating something important.

"What're we gonna do about her?" one woman asked nervously.

A man with a dark beard standing nearby replied, "Well, we've come all the way out here. We've got to make sure we take care of this. She can't threaten our children! We're all better off if she's left out here. No one'll ever find her. That's fer sure."

Another man grunted in agreement.

"Yep. We've gotta be strong. She's evil. There's no other way."

The group murmured in agreement and, to Roy's surprise, started walking back into the woods.

To his shock, they disappeared.

Into thin air.

"What the hell?" he whispered.

The calming buzzing feeling disappeared, and he was now confused and lost.

Roy stumbled into the clearing and was stunned to see the bonfire disappear. He was now standing in front of a set of charred rocks and ash.

Fear began to set in, and Roy stumbled back with the realization that he was lost in the middle of the woods and had no idea how he'd gotten there. He had no cell phone and no way to get in touch with anyone.

And it was getting dark.

CHAPTER 5

When Brett emerged from the cabin, he was frustrated to see that Roy was gone. But he wasn't completely surprised. His friend had been acting strangely ever since they'd left Carrie and Anita at the cabin.

Instinctively, Brett looked down at his watch. He was shocked to see how late it was, and had a feeling that sunset was on its way, if it hadn't arrived already.

The sky was a dark shade of purple, indicating the arrival of nightfall.

Brett remembered Jack's reminder that they not be wandering around in the middle of the night. So he looked for the trail and began to retrace his steps.

Roy's probably back at the cabin already, he thought.

Looking back towards Cabin B, Brett shuddered. He wasn't sure what the hair he'd found had been attached to, but it seemed as if something was under the floorboards and he could only imagine what dead animals might be lying under the wooden slats.

But you don't think it's animal hair, do you? You think there's someone underneath that floor, don't you?

Trying to shake the voices from his mind, Brett turned and began quickly walking back to his group's cabin. His heart was still racing in his chest and sweat was now freely traveling down his face in small rivers, but he forced himself to think rationally.

"I'm fine, no need to panic," he mumbled to himself as he began to retrace his steps through the darkening woods.

It seemed to take forever, but he was finally able to make out their small cabin in the distance, due in large part to the light that they'd left on by the front door. It was like a beacon guiding him back after a rough day out at sea, and Brett could feel his entire body loosen up in relief.

As he climbed the steps, he took a deep breath and tried to calm himself. It wouldn't do any good to walk into the cabin like a huge jumble of nerves. That would only stress the girls out and given that Anita didn't seem to be feeling all that well earlier, he needed to stay calm.

So he focused on appearing relaxed and reached for the front door, pushing it open slowly. To his surprise, most of the inside lights were off, with the exception of some small table lamps.

"Carrie? Anita? I'm back," he called out.

"We're in here," Carrie said from one of the bedrooms.

Brett could see a light shining from the bedroom that Anita and Roy were sharing. But it wasn't a bright light either; it was another bedside lamp that had been turned on.

That's strange. Why are all the lights off?

As Brett entered the bedroom, he initially turned away. The room smelled horrible, like rotting meat.

When he turned back to the women, his breath caught in his throat.

Anita was lying on the pillow, her eyes staring at the ceiling. But her entire face was glistening and red. She looked swollen, and her skin was bleeding in many places.

Brett looked down at the stained bed sheets, and tried not to gag.

"What the hell?" he asked, not able to construct a full sentence. He couldn't understand how Anita had gotten so bad within the past hour. When he'd left the cabin she'd looked fine. Maybe a little sick, but nothing like this.

Carrie stood up from the bed. "Anita, I'm just going to talk to Brett outside for a minute. Will you be ok?"

"Yes," she whispered.

Pulling Brett out of the room, Carrie stood in the hallway, concern clearly painted across her face.

"We've got to get her out of here. She's really sick."

"Yeah, I can see that. What happened?"

Carrie reached over and turned on the hallway light so that she could get a better look at Brett and realized that he didn't look great, either.

"Are you ok?" she asked.

"I'm fine. Just tell me what happened here."

Carrie went through the events of the past hour and hesitantly included her own story about passing out in the bathroom. When she shared with Brett the image she'd seen in the mirror, her breath caught in her throat and tears threatened.

"I'm so scared. What the hell was that?"

Brett wasn't sure.

Animal hair? Or human hair?

Carrie was continuing to talk, but his thoughts were elsewhere. What if the hair in the cabin and what Carrie had seen were connected? What if there was some sort of woman underneath the floorboards? Shouldn't they alert the authorities?

What authorities? We're in the middle of the damned woods.

"Brett, are you listening to me?"

He snapped back to present day and could tell that Carrie was starting to get frustrated.

"Sorry—go ahead. I'm listening."

She shook her blonde hair in annoyance and then started again. "I think we need to carry Anita back to the car and get her to the hospital. She may not make it through the night. At the rate she's going, the bacteria may shut down her entire system."

"You really think she has this flesh-eating disease?"

Carrie nodded. "Yeah, I do. She looks just like all the photos I've seen. And it gets worse, Brett. She's deteriorating so fast that it won't take long for her entire body to go into shock. We've got to get her out of here. By the way, where's Roy?"

"He didn't come back before me?"

"No. We haven't seen him all afternoon. Once you guys left that was the last time we saw him. Where is he?"

Brett felt concern race through his veins. "I'm not sure. We took a walk through the woods to look for the other cabin, and when I went inside, he stayed outside. Then, when I came back, he was gone."

Carrie's face hardened, "Why'd you go in?"

"Well, we just wanted to see if anyone was staying there. It was stupid, anyway. The place was empty."

Brett wasn't comfortable lying to Carrie, but she seemed irritated with him, and he didn't want to make things worse. In addition, he needed to figure out a way to get Anita some help and bringing up his own frightening experience wouldn't make things better. So he figured that keeping things quiet for now would be best.

"How are we going to get her back to the car?" Carrie pressed.

He wasn't sure. The darkness had now completely overtaken the park and if they were to try to carry her to the car, it could take them a while. Plus, he wasn't even sure if she could walk. For a minute, he imagined a helicopter hovering over the park and somehow finding a way to land amid the tall trees and uneven terrain. It was a ridiculous thought, and he smiled.

"What's so funny?" Carrie asked, her annoyance now clearly identifiable in the tone of her voice.

"Sorry. I was just thinking we could really use a helipad right now. But that's not gonna happen, so what if I go down to the office and see if there's a way for me to get my car up here? Maybe there's some kind of paved road that we just didn't see. Parks usually have these kind of roads so that they can navigate through quickly in an emergency or make deliveries. What do you think?"

Carrie wasn't sure she wanted to be in the cabin alone with Anita while Brett trekked through the dark. It was extremely creepy outside and with Roy still missing, she didn't know how they could leave until they found him.

Still, Anita was getting worse, and if they just stood around and waited for Roy to return, his girlfriend might not make it.

And don't forget about the witch in the mirror, a little voice whispered in her ear.

Carrie shivered and rubbed her arms for comfort. There was no easy answer to Brett's question, but she knew that the best thing to do was to be brave and wait in the cabin until he returned with help.

"Ok, I'll wait here while you go get help. Hopefully he's still in his office."

"Yeah, Ranger Jack Blaze. Mr. Personality. This should be fun." Brett chuckled, trying to lighten the mood. "Wish my damned cell phone worked. If we had internet or cell service, we could at least call or text someone. Guess I've gotta do things the old fashioned way."

As they walked toward the door, Carrie stopped.

Brett turned around, confused.

"I'm scared," she whispered.

He reached out and pulled her into his arms for an embrace. They clung to each other and fear of the unknown settled on their shoulders.

Around them, the dust continued to swirl and dance along the countertops and tables. No one noticed that it had begun to form little piles in the corners and crevices.

CHAPTER 6

The woods were now completely dark, and Roy was using the moonlight to help guide him so that he didn't trip and break his neck. Somehow he'd stumbled onto some rough terrain, and the ground was uneven in many spots.

He found himself carefully navigating through miniature cliffs and hills that appeared to be on an incline.

The winds had quieted down and part of him wished that the buzzing in his ears would return. He was doing everything in his power to not panic, but the truth was that he was in the middle of the woods with no cell service, no flashlight, nothing. And instead of listening to the advice they'd been given, he was screwed—stuck in the middle of the woods with no one to help him.

After the group in the clearing had disappeared, he'd been unsuccessful in finding them again. He'd actually called out a few times into the darkness, hoping that they'd stop. But he'd been met with silence. Roy wondered if they'd actually been real at all, or if he'd just been hallucinating due to the stress of getting lost in the wilderness.

There's got to be an easier way back. If I can just find the lake, I can find my way back from there.

Suddenly he heard murmurings in the distance and turned to follow the sounds. His shoes crunched against the leaves and rocks as he navigated through the woods. Roy tried to protect his face and arms from getting completely destroyed by the sharp branches that continued to assault him, but it wasn't easy, and he could feel his skin tear from the teeth of the biting bark.

The sounds grew louder and to Roy's surprise, he found

himself near Cabin B, where he'd started out nearly an hour before. He was hopeful that this would help him retrace the path back to the cabin where the rest of his group was staying.

They're probably worried sick about me. I'll bet Anita is bitching up a storm.

As he drew closer to the cabin, he saw a group of people standing outside. It was the same group he'd seen standing around the bonfire in the clearing.

Roy watched them. It was a bunch of men and woman—a total of six couples. Some of them carried flashlights, and they all seemed nervous.

Roy crept closer and listened in.

"Ok," the man with the beard said to the rest of the group. "We've got to do this now. If any of y'all aren't interested in going any further, then leave now. Ya hear?"

The members of the group murmured in agreement and no one walked away. This seemed to please the man, who appeared to be one of the leaders of the group.

"Ok, let's go."

It was at this moment when Roy realized that there was a light on in the cabin. He wasn't sure how he'd missed it during his trek over, but now he could clearly see a yellow glow in the window and smoke coming out of the chimney.

What the hell?

As Roy watched, he could see the group file inside and a woman's voice greet them. There were sounds of talking going on within and then all of a sudden a loud crash erupted. The noise cut through the silent night and set his nerves on edge.

He could see a scuffle happening through the window as the woman inside was seized by two of the men, who then proceeded to drag her outside.

Roy backed away, not wanting to be seen by the group— he was getting a bad feeling that he might not be welcome by these people who were clearly trespassing and assaulting an unarmed citizen.

Once outside, the woman screeched at them, her voice thin and grating.

"You can't do this to me! I haven't done anything to ya.

Leave me alone or you'll suffer. All of ya!"

The bearded man laughed at her. "You bitch. You've done us wrong already. We want you out of here, or we'll make sure you leave."

The woman glared at him and then stopped struggling. She smiled in the moonlight, and Roy could see that her teeth were jagged and dirty.

She wasn't an attractive woman and looked to be about fifty or so. It was difficult for Roy to see the color of her hair in the darkness, but it was frizzy and stuck out all over. She was wearing a dirty white dress that was tattered and fell past her knees.

"I know you," she sneered at her captor, spittle flying from her lips. "You ain't satisfied by your wife, so you pull out your small cock and stroke it any chance you get. How does it feel to cum while yer watching the teenage girls outside, eh?"

She screeched and laughed at her own joke while the bearded man backed away a few steps—obviously caught off guard.

"You don't know what yer talking about," he said, a bit less confident than before. "And you best keep your damned mouth shut. We all know you've been practicing witchcraft in your house and killing off our animals. Ever since you came to the mountain you've been nothing but trouble. It's time for you to go."

The strange woman laughed again, and Roy could feel the tiny hairs on his arms stand up.

"I ain't leaving. You'll have to kill me first. But be warned— touch me, and I'll be makin sure you never forget it for the rest of yer miserable lives."

"Oh, let's just leave 'er alone," one of the women said, her shaky voice indicating that she was on the verge of tears.

"Yeh, maybe this ain't such a good idea. She's fucking batshit anyway," another man said in agreement.

"No. We gotta do this. She's dangerous. If you ain't with me, get the hell outta here," said the bearded man, contempt oozing from his words.

To Roy's surprise, the two people who'd spoken up turned

and left together. For a second, he considered following them, but they were headed in the opposite direction, and he eventually needed to get back to his own cabin. So he sat tight and remained hidden behind the trees.

"Anyone else feel like leaving? This is yer last chance. So don't fuck around."

No one else in the group moved and the captive woman cackled once more.

"You're all gonna die here. I'll curse ya and make damned sure yer lives are nothing but black pits of Hell. And then when I'm done with ya, you'll find yourself trapped the same way yer trapping me."

"Shut up, you dumb bitch," the bearded man said, but his voice was wavering and he seemed nervous. Without warning, he pushed the woman into the woods.

The group murmured as they filed out into the darkness of the trees and away from the house.

Roy wondered where they were going and decided to follow behind them. He was far enough away that he wouldn't be discovered, but he also made sure that he moved quickly enough to still see the yellow glow from their flashlights.

As he crept along, he worried about finding his way back.

It looks like I'll need to borrow one of their flashlights. But I can't just leave that poor woman. Somehow I've got to figure out what the hell is going on.

The group of people finally stopped at another clearing. The men and women were visibly nervous now and whispered to each other as their bearded companion prodded the captive woman forward.

She'd been silent on their walk, which Roy found strange. He tried to lean against a tree and watch the spectacle in front of him, when he noticed that one of his feet had begun to sink into the ground.

"What the hell?" he asked, and then realized that he'd made too much noise.

Quickly pulling his sinking foot from the mud, he backed away and crouched behind a tree stump, his heart beating fast in his chest.

Did they hear me? Panic began to seep into his veins. He remained absolutely still for a few terrifying seconds.

Thankfully, the people didn't seem to notice him at all.

I'd better be careful. The ground is like quicksand around here.

Just then, a voice cut through the night air and pierced the darkness like a needle.

It was the bearded man and he instructed all of the people he was with to stand in a circle, surrounding the woman from the cabin.

"Now you gotta face the consequences," he bellowed. "You took our animals and planned to hurt our kids. Yer a witch. This is the only way."

The woman looked at him and then spit on the ground.

"I ain't done nothing," she said. "I've kept to myself and only taken what I needed for food. Yer gonna pay for this. All of ya."

To Roy's horror, as she said the words, her body began to sink.

The woman was going to sink into the ground and die.

Roy's legs sprang to life and he ran directly into the circle of people. "Stop! You've gotta let her go. She's going to die. You can't do this!"

But to his surprise, as soon as he bolted into the clearing, the group disappeared and he was left with the sinking woman. He reached out to try to grab her hand, but his fingers passed right through her arm.

"You dumb little boy," she laughed. "It's too late. You'd better run."

Her mouth widened as she laughed and the sound seemed to travel through the wind, weaving a web of terror around Roy's head.

Something in his mind snapped and he turned and ran back into the woods.

CHAPTER 7

Carrie watched as Brett set off into the woods armed with a flashlight. She felt frightened and helpless and didn't want to be left alone with Anita. But there was no choice. The woman was too sick to make the trek back to the car, so somebody had to wait with her.

And there was no phone or internet service.

She was stuck.

It wasn't that Carrie didn't like taking care of sick people. She'd been instrumental in caring for her younger sister most of her childhood. Having two working parents and a sibling with Asperger syndrome, Carrie was familiar with patience and having to deal with people who needed her.

But this was different.

There was something strange about Anita's condition. It was progressing too rapidly and the severity of the symptoms was something she'd never read about in any of her textbooks. Typically it took a day or so for the situation to truly worsen.

Anita had fallen ill within *hours*.

"Hello?" a feeble voice called out from the other room.

"I'm coming," responded Carrie.

As she walked back into the bedroom, a terrible smell assuaged her nostrils. It smelled like the worst unwashed body odor she'd ever come across.

Anita was still lying in the bed, but she had turned her body away and was facing the wall. She was shaking and Carrie could tell that the woman was crying.

"Honey, what's wrong?"

"Something's really wrong. I can't feel my face anymore,

and it's getting hard to see."

Carrie reached out and touched Anita's shoulder. "Turn over and let me see."

Anita turned over, and Carrie nearly passed out.

The woman's entire face had turned into a mass of oozing, red pus. Pieces of skin were falling off now in strips, and some were barely hanging on. To make matters worse, Anita's eyes were red and watery, liquid dripping from the corner of each orb.

It was something out of a horror movie, and Carrie wasn't initially sure how to react. She wondered how to help ease the woman's pain while they waited for Brett to return.

"I think we need to wash off your face and put something on your sores so that they don't get infected. Can you try to make it into the bathroom?"

"I'm not sure. Don't have any energy," Anita mumbled.

Carrie ignored Anita's weak response and took one of her hands gingerly. She could see sores beginning to appear all up and down the woman's arms and hands and didn't want to inadvertently create any more damage.

Anita struggled to sit up and was finally able to sit in an upright position with her back against the wall. She then swung her legs over the side of the bed and carefully stood up.

Carrie slowly led her to the bathroom and was careful to block the mirror with her body so that Anita couldn't see how awful she'd become. She helped the woman sit down on the toilet seat and then rushed over to the sink to soak one of the hand towels in some cool water.

She made sure to avoid the mirror, not wanting to possibly come in contact again with the old woman who'd been leering at her from its reflection.

"Am I going to die?" Anita asked in a small voice.

Carrie quickly wrung out the towel and knelt down in front of the sick woman. She managed to keep from reacting to the sight in front of her and carefully dabbed the Anita's face with the cloth.

"No, you're not going to die. You're going to be fine."

The sick woman began to sob. "No, no. I'm not fine.

Everything hurts, and it feels like my skin is sliding off. I'm burning. It's like I'm on fire but there's no flame."As Anita put her head down and sobbed, flakes of skin continued to slide off and drops of blood dripped onto the wooden floor.

It was a horrible, yet fascinating sight, and for a moment Carrie lost herself as she watched the blood dot the floor like an obscure work of art.

It's so weird. It looks like a strange painting. If another drop of blood hits that spot over there, it will make a face. See? Eyes, a small nose— now all she needs is a mouth. Come on, just one more drop.

The woods were dark and unfamiliar, making it difficult for Brett to retrace his steps. His flashlight was helping him follow the smooth path that had led them to their cabin, but every so often, he found himself taking a wrong step and stumbling over rocks and branches. In addition, the weather was uncomfortably warm, and a quick gust of wind would blow through every once in a while, moaning as it traveled through the night air.

Brett wondered about Roy. His friend had been gone for a few hours and he hoped that everything was all right. Roy wasn't someone to typically wander around in the dark, but perhaps he'd found some fun vacationers staying in one of the cabins and had stopped for a beer or two. The man wasn't well equipped to handle stress, and with the way Anita had been behaving lately, it wasn't a mystery as to why he'd chosen to disappear for a bit.

Still, it was quite inconvenient, because they needed to leave and find medical help. Brett had never seen anyone look as sick as Anita, though he remembered a movie he'd watched several years back about a woman who died out in the woods because of a flesh-eating disease. The situation seemed similar, but he wasn't an actor in a movie.

This was real, and his friend's girlfriend could actually die.

Picking up his pace, Brett continued on until he saw the cabin he and Roy had visited earlier. A chill raced through his veins, and he tried to ignore the structure and just walk on past—but something caught his eye.

As he tried to casually glance over, he felt as if his heart had stopped beating.

There was a light on in the cabin.

"What the hell?" he whispered.

As he moved closer to the cabin, he could see that there were at least two lights glowing inside. The first one was in the main living room area, and the other one was sending a warm light through the window of what he could only imagine was one of the bedrooms.

Did I leave the lights on earlier? he wondered.

Brett tried to think back to when he'd walked through the cabin. He couldn't recall whether or not he'd turned on any of the lights, but he started to worry that if he had it was wasting a lot of electricity.

Seriously? Am I really standing out here debating whether or not to turn off those lights? I've gotta find help.

But even while his mind was arguing with him to be rational and seek help, Brett's legs were guiding him in the direction of the cabin. There was a growing curiosity in his mind and the morbid memory of the hair that was sticking up through the slat in the floorboard continued to burn in his brain.

He knew he was making a mistake, could feel it in every cell within his body, but he still …

… couldn't keep himself from walking up to the cabin.

As Brett stood outside, he put his head close to the door to see if he could hear any sounds from inside the structure, but everything was quiet.

Almost *too* quiet.

He decided to knock on the door—just in case.

"Hello? Is anyone inside?"

Silence.

He knocked louder.

"Hello? I'm coming in."

Brett felt ridiculous and wondered if he had completely lost his mind.

Ok, this is nuts. But if there's someone inside, maybe they can help me get some assistance faster. Maybe they've got a car somewhere close by.

He reached out and slowly turned the doorknob, hearing

the hinges creak as the door swung open. Brett stood in the doorway for a moment and looked inside.

A lamp that was situated by a large couch was shining brightly, sending a white-yellow cast across the room. The rest of the living room and the kitchen were dark.

"Hello? Is there anyone in here?"

Brett heard a chuckle. It seemed to have come from the bedroom and was barely audible, even in the stillness of the night.

"Hello? Is there someone in here? I need help. One of our friends is sick, and I've got to get back to the ranger's office quickly."

Thump.

Brett could feel panic begin to rise in his throat and he fought back the urge to scream.

"Is anyone there?"

Silence.

Taking a deep breath, Brett walked toward the light. He found himself taking careful steps and slowly putting one foot in front of the other, as if each step was taking him closer to a fate worse than death. He didn't want to proceed forward, but he felt like there was an invisible force luring him in closer and closer.

I'm like a moth drawn to a flame.

Brett finally made it to the doorway of the bedroom and stood for a moment, almost afraid to look in. As he shakily peered around the corner, he could see that a woman was sitting on the bed with her back to him.

She was facing the wall and slowly rocking back and forth. Her hair was wild and uncombed, and she was wearing a white peasant dress that was creased and dirty.

"Ma'am, excuse me. Are you ok?" he asked.

She didn't answer and continued rocking back and forth.

A million horror movies flashed through his mind, and Brett knew that the best thing to do was to run far, far away. But somehow he'd lost control of his better judgment and wasn't listening to his senses anymore. The night had gotten so out of control that he was simply following along as it carried him deeper and deeper into its insanities.

As he neared the edge of the bed, the woman stopped rocking.

"What do ya want?" she asked in a strained voice.

Brett thought she sounded old and tired, but there was also something else in her tone.

Something threatening.

He cleared his throat and tried to keep his voice from trembling. "Sorry to bother you, but my friend's very sick, and I was wondering if you have a car or a way to quickly get to the front gate?"

The woman chuckled dryly.

"No, I ain't got no car, honey. And yer friend's not gonna get better anytime soon."

Brett wasn't sure what to say, so he just stood in place.

"Ya see, everyone's always looking for what I can do fer them, but what has anyone ever done fer me? Nothing! That's what I say. Nothing! And now, yer all gonna pay."

She laughed again, and Brett started backing up.

"Um, thanks for the advice," he said as he began moving away from the strange woman.

The woman started stroking her hair. "Ya like my hair, honey? Yeah, I saw you earlier. How's about you eat some of it for me?"

She laughed out loud and then slowly turned around.

Brett finally found the strength in his legs and turned to run out of the cabin. But before his body fully twisted in the other direction, he caught sight of the woman's face.

The woman looked as if she was in her late fifties or early sixties, but she definitely wasn't alive anymore. Her eyes were completely black, and her skin was gray and mottled. She was decaying, but somehow she was still moving, speaking, and … laughing.

She began laughing louder and louder as Brett fled and ran back into the woods.

He pushed past the bushes and ran into the forest as fast as his legs would carry him. To his horror, he could still hear her laughter, and as he turned quickly to look back, he could see that the woman had exited the cabin and was making her way into the woods as well.

Shit! She's chasing me!

Brett doubled down and sprinted at full speed. The scenery passed him on both sides as he raced at a rate he didn't even think was possible.

Roy was unable to move another inch. Every cell in his body ached, and it felt nearly impossible for him to catch his breath. He'd been running for nearly a half hour and couldn't seem to find his way out.

He wasn't sure how big Sunken Park was, but it seemed like it ran for miles on end. And no matter how long he walked or ran, the scenery all looked the same around him. He kept looking for the lake or the front gates or anything that would give him an indication of where he was.

But there was nothing around that looked familiar, while at the same time everything looked the same. All of the trees seemed to be slanting in the same direction, the same cluster of bushes would appear every few minutes, and everything was just so dense and wooded.

To top it off, Roy was hungry, thirsty, and monumentally aggravated.

He was also scared and afraid that he might die in the midst of the nightmare woods he found himself wandering through. In fact, his mind was beginning to swirl and blaze with irrational thoughts of starvation or dehydration or worse.

It was at that exact moment, when he thought all was lost … when the buzzing voice returned.

The words were whispered into his ear like velvet water and instantly had a calming effect.

Come find us. We're here. You're safe here with us.

Almost immediately Roy felt the tension in his muscles evaporate, and his blood pressure began to drop as a pleasant, hazy feeling overtook his mind and body.

He slowly stood up and without realizing it, began swaying back and forth. The voice was so elegant and relaxing that it had created a strange music within his mind, and his body was simply reacting to the pitch and cadence of the sounds.

After a few moments, Roy's feet began to lead him in a particular direction. Even though he wasn't sure where he was going, he was comfortable in the fact that his body was following the right path. And the voice was there to guide him every step of the way.

Come this way, it cooed. *Follow me this way. It will all be right when you get there. There's no fighting or stress with us. Just relax and become a part of our energy. Our soil.*

To Roy's surprise, he was beginning to feel sexually aroused and was amazed that his penis was beginning to harden as he moved slowly through the woods. He reached down and tugged on himself mechanically because it felt so good. He couldn't believe how great he was feeling. It was as if sweet sensations were dripping down on him and traveling all the way to his feet.

Damn, it feels like I'm on ecstasy.

He continued to float through the woods until he found himself in a medium-sized clearing.

In the center of the clearing was a naked woman standing under the moonlight. She had wild hair and was as pale as snow, her skin almost glowing against the bluish rays of the moon.

Roy felt himself get even harder. He wanted nothing more than to feel the woman's softness against his shaft. He could imagine her providing him sweet relief like a pool of cold water to satisfy his burning sexuality.

Without even providing an introduction, he moved toward her, his trance fully taking over every aspect of his mind. His erection was so powerful now that he began rubbing himself continually, not even caring that this strange woman would see him pleasuring himself.

He moved so that he was standing right in front of her and looked at a beautiful, youthful face that gazed at him curiously.

The woman had large eyes, a petite mouth, and the whitest skin he'd ever seen. She was beautiful and pure.

He wanted her.

Immediately.

Roy reached out to touch her arm, but instead of connecting

with the skin that he could only imagine was soft and plush, his hand passed through her. He stumbled forward and fell to the ground.

When he regained his stability, Roy looked around.

The woman was gone, and he was alone in the woods.

And now the voice was gone, too.

Suddenly, the earth beneath him shifted and he began to sink into the soil.

"Crap!" he shouted. "Hey, someone help me. I'm in trouble!"

But no one answered, and Roy realized that he was on his own. He'd have to find a way out somehow.

The ground was now giving way more quickly, and Roy's feet had already been pulled under. He was sinking fast and was already knee-deep in the muck. There wasn't much time to lose.

Looking around quickly, Roy saw a tree root sticking out of the ground and strained to grab a hold of it. He pulled forward with as much strength as he could, but to his horror, the more he struggled, the faster his body sank down.

He was now waist-deep in the mud.

Panic began to bubble up, but Roy forced it down and tried to think of a way out. He looked around and decided that there was nothing he could do but try to wade through the muck and crawl out when he reached a safe spot.

Roy tried to push his way forward so that he could get out of the dirt that was trying to pull him under. He was able to move a few inches when his right foot lost all traction and sank down.

The mud rose up on all sides and Roy could feel the muck filling his ears and mouth as his entire body sank down. Choking and sputtering, he was able to push himself up for a quick second and gasped for breath.

"Help!" he choked.

But within a few moments, the muck won the battle and his entire body was pulled down into the ground.

Roy's eyes went blind immediately as the mud covered his fragile orbs with a brown-black film and his lungs eventually sucked in the dirt concoction.

As his life faded, there was a moment when his dying mind connected with the image of the woman he'd seen in the clearing. She seemed older now, and not as pretty. Her clothes were torn and simple and he realized that he was staring at the same woman who'd been taken prisoner and forced out of her house.

The woman who'd been killed and who had suffered the same fate that he was facing now.

She smiled, blew him a kiss, and then faded from view.

As the last of Roy disappeared under the earth, the trees maintained their stillness and the world was calm and cruel.

CHAPTER 8

Anita was scared shitless.

She didn't want to die, but she wasn't sure she'd make it through the night. Her entire body was on fire, the fatigue was getting worse, and she could feel her heart beating quickly in her chest. Every so often, she'd get a strange racing sensation as if the rhythm of her heartbeat was out of sync.

Meanwhile, her skin was falling off in disgusting clumps, she was oozing from every limb, and the skin she did have felt horribly itchy. But she didn't want to scratch anything because it exacerbated the bleeding and oozing.

To make matters worse, Carrie was acting weird. She was sitting on the bathroom floor, staring at the ground, and murmuring all sorts of strange things.

Anita had tried to get the woman to snap out of it, but nothing worked.

Carrie seemed almost catatonic.

"To hell with this," Anita mumbled and stood up slowly. It was painful to walk, but if she stayed in the bathroom, she might entirely melt away.

Kinda like the wicked witch in The Wizard of Oz, she thought. The idea struck her as quite funny, and she chuckled to herself.

I must be losing my mind. Here I am, basically disintegrating, and I'm laughing like a lunatic. I'm melting!

The phrase reminded her of The Wizard of Oz once more and she broke out in giggles. It hurt to laugh, but she felt a little better with some humor to lean on. In fact, the laughter gave Anita additional courage, and she began to consider leaving the cabin and finding her way out.

If I stay here, I'm definitely not going to make it. Carrie's turned into a fucking lunatic and god knows where Brett is. And where the hell is Roy? If I ever survive this, I'm gonna dump his ass first chance I get!

Avoiding her reflection in the kitchen window, Anita found her flip-flops by the dishwasher and carefully put them on by sliding a foot into each shoe. The mere activity caused intense pain and some more skin to peel off, but she did her best to ignore it.

Taking a deep breath, she slowly shuffled forward and was able to get from the kitchen to the front door. Anita grasped the knob tightly, pushed the door open, and peered outside.

The night was dark and still. There were no lights in the distance and everything was eerily quiet.

She debated her options.

Do I go out there? It's so dark. I'll need a flashlight. Wait, there's one by the couch. Ouch. Ok, I've got it. It's not the biggest flashlight in the world, but it should work. Damn, am I really going to go out there? Everything hurts so badly, and I can barely keep my thoughts straight.

Carrie moaned from the bathroom.

I can't stay here with her. She's going to make things worse. Ok, I'm going to do it. It's now or never.

Anita took a deep breath and turned on the flashlight. Limping forward, she aimed the thin stream of light in front of her and made her way into the woods.

Brett stopped at a tree and hunched forward, trying to catch his breath. He'd never been so scared in his life and would be perfectly happy if he never stepped foot inside a cabin again. The memory of the strange hag he'd seen was both terrifying and perplexing.

Who was she? And why was she so angry?

He wondered about the Sunken Park pamphlet they'd picked up in the restaurant and his initial reservations. He'd had a bad feeling about it and now it was too late. They were all stuck inside some horrible place that was dark and strange.

And dangerous?

A glint of light caught Brett's eye and he was relieved to see that there was a lake off to his right. He remembered that they had passed a small body of water on the way to the cabin, so he was probably less than a mile from the front gates.

Picking up his pace, he kept moving and focused all of his concentration on keeping his legs from giving way. His entire body felt achy, as if he'd been up for days instead of just one night. His muscles, particularly his calves, felt like they were cramping up. And his breath wasn't quite pulling into his lungs as much as he needed, causing him to pant and wheeze as he quickly made his way through the woods.

Still, he focused all of his energy on the park ranger's office and finally made his way to a larger clearing and could see the small office building ahead.

With his last reserve of energy, Brett picked up the pace and started running toward the structure. He tried calling out as he ran, but his voice was hoarse and came out as a mere whisper.

"Help. Please help me."

As he got closer to the building, his foot caught on a stone, and his entire body fell forward into the grass. The flashlight tumbled from his grasp and rolled on the ground, finally resting on a cluster of rocks that ended up propping up its front end so that it was casting a weak glow against the building.

Brett moaned and got up slowly, dusting off his arms and legs. He felt like a fool for falling, but as his eyes focused on the light cast from the flashlight, his mind quickly shifted into another gear, because he was staring at something not quite possible.

The building hadn't moved or changed size or anything strange like that. It was even worse.

The building looked *old*.

The walls were cracked, and there were small weeds sprouting out of the fissures like unshaven hairs on an elderly man's face. There was dirt caked along the white concrete, and the windows were cloudy with thin cracks along the surface. The roof was missing tiles in different places, and the back door was boarded up with wood.

"This can't be right," Brett said out loud.

He walked around to the front doorway and was astonished

to see that there wasn't a door at all, but rather an open space with a broken chain-link barrier lying on the ground. When he picked up the chain, it contained a worn sign that read:

"Building Condemned By Order Of The County. No Trespassing. Trespassers Will Be Prosecuted To The Fullest Extent Of The Law."

Brett tossed the sign aside and walked into the building.

"Hello? Ranger Blaze? Anyone?"

Silence.

And then—the sound of something rustling.

With a trembling hand, Brett held out the flashlight in front of him and carefully walked through the building.

It was a small structure, with a long hallway that led all the way to the back wall and had rooms accessible from each side. In the front by the entrance, there was a small waiting area with a few dusty old chairs and a desk, presumably where a receptionist used to sit.

He began to make his way down the hallway and angled his flashlight so that it was shining inside the first room. The door was propped open and was hanging from one hinge. Inside there were a number of supplies like hoses, other old flashlights, tarps, and tools. Boxes were piled high against the wall, and dust swirled softly against the alien light.

Brett thought about going inside and sifting through the boxes, but then decided against it because he didn't want to come into contact with any bugs or strange creatures.

He went back into the hallway and crossed over to the other side where there was another room. This one looked like an office, and contained a few desks that were covered with old papers, notebooks, and ledgers.

The ledger on top of one of the desks had the words "Sunken Park Financials" handwritten on the cover and as Brett leafed through it, he could see that it contained figures of different park purchases and expenses.

He flipped to the last page of the notebook and frowned.

The last date that had been logged was 11/12/89.

As in 1989? That's a really long time ago. What the hell is going on here?

Brett put the notebook aside and continued flipping through the pile. He pulled out a thin piece of paper that looked like an old police report. It was a copy because the ink looked faded and unoriginal, and as he read through it, the blood in his veins began to turn icy:

"April 1, 1989

Time: 13:45

Details: Body of Caucasian woman in her mid-fifties pulled from northwestern point of park perimeter. Appears to have no body trauma. Rigor Mortis fully apparent. Skin free from wounds. Death estimated at least several days ago.
Cause of Death: Accidental suffocation."

The rest of the report was smudged by a coffee stain that extended from the middle to the bottom of the paper.
Brett put it down and continued leafing through the material. He found a piece of paper that was smaller than the rest and recognized it as a newspaper article. Holding the flashlight close to the yellowed paper, he read the news brief:

"April 2, 1989

Georgia State Police have discovered the body of a woman just outside a local park in Pine Mountain, Georgia.
According to authorities, the woman apparently got lost in the woods in the middle of the night and stumbled into a mud trap. She became disoriented and drowned.
The woman, Sandra Nunkes, was a longtime resident of Pine Mountain and lived in a cabin near the park. Authorities had been called to Nunkes' house recently due to an argument between the woman and other local residents.
Sources say they'd been arguing about a rash of missing animals that Nunkes was accused of stealing. Authorities did not make any arrests at the time, but did issue a citation to the woman after finding several dead animals on the premises.

Locals have been questioned in connection with the deceased, but no arrests have been made.

The park has been closed until the investigation can be completed."

Brett reread the article several times, but no matter how many times he looked at it, he was having a difficult time absorbing the facts. As he stared at the name of the woman who'd died in the park, he easily rearranged the letters of her last name.

When the letters were rearranged, Nunkes spelled "Sunken."

Woah. Is that a coincidence? Weird.

Putting down the newspaper article, Brett continued to shuffle through the papers on the desk, hoping to uncover something else. But all he could find were purchase orders and receipts.

He walked back into the hallway and was about to continue into the next room, when he heard the slight rustling sound again. Brett took a deep breath, trying to prepare himself for whatever waited. Standing behind the wall near the doorway, he called out, "Is anyone there? I've got a gun."

Brett had never owned a gun in his life, but figured now was not the time to be all about peace and love. If there was something or someone in the building with him, he had no doubt that it was planning on harming him in some way..

Brett carefully peeked around the corner. A whoosh of breath released itself from his mouth when he saw what was causing the rustling sound.

The room was full of paper and trash. A hole in the window was allowing the wind to blow through, and the occasional gust sent the papers dancing in a circular fashion on the dusty ground. There was dust everywhere it seemed, and the air was thick with a musty smell of age and wear.

Brett coughed, and then walked into the room. He eyed the papers on the floor and then looked at the walls.

There were photographs adorning the different sections of the room. Some of them were extremely outdated, with the men in the photographs wearing suits from the seventies and sporting hairdos that were of a different era.

Brett shined his flashlight toward the bottom of each portrait, where an engraved silver plaque resided. The plaques were on each frame, so he figured it was some sort of historical set of images. When his flashlight finally hit the words on the metal, he could see that each plaque read, "Pine Mountain Elk Ranger," with a consecutive year inscribed on its smooth surface.

As he looked at the different faces that stared back at him, one stood out more than the others. It was the portrait at the furthermost point of the room and the last one in the series. Brett approached it cautiously, acid churning in his stomach at the realization that things were very, very wrong.

The photograph was of Ranger Jack Blaze. He looked identical to when they'd last seen him, with the exception of the fact that he sported a full beard in the picture. There was, however, one little problem.

The photo was from 1989.

It was now 2014.

CHAPTER 9

Carrie wasn't sure how long she'd been sitting on the ground. Her head hurt, her back was on fire, and her eyes felt dry and grainy. To make matters worse, when she'd come to her senses, she found herself staring at an array of red splotches that she could only assume were dried drops of blood.

Groaning, she hoisted herself up into a standing position and remained upright for a moment while spots swam before her eyes. The room seemed to tilt and sway and then slowly came to a standstill.

Carrie gingerly looked around the small bathroom and was concerned when she didn't see Anita anywhere.

"Anita, are you ok?"

There was no answer, and her voice seemed to reverberate through the cabin. It was at this exact moment, when Carrie noticed that there was quite a bit of dust on her hands and clothing. Shuddering, she wiped herself down, trying to get some of the white, web-like filth off of her body.

Gross, she thought. *I don't remember seeing so much dirt when we first got here. I must've been too into Brett to realize.*

As she walked out of the bathroom, a warm wind swept through, rustling her hair. Carrie then noticed that the cabin's front door was wide open, an inky blackness seeping through the open space.

"Oh shit."

She made her way to the doorway and looked out into the night. Carrie could hear crickets chirping in the distance and felt the warmth of the night rest against her cheeks and forehead. It was extremely dark, and it was hard for her to see anything more than a few yards away.

The light from inside the cabin reflected against the nearby trees, making them appear strong and menacing.

"Anita!" Carrie called out, hoping that the woman had just gone outside for some fresh air.

But no one answered, and her mind began to race.

What the hell do I do now?

She knew that Anita was too sick to get very far. The woman was battling a strange, powerful bacteria that was eating her alive. Carrie knew from her nursing studies that flesh-eating bacteria didn't stop at the flesh. It destroyed everything, including muscles and organs. And if that was what was inflicting Anita, the woman was in a race against time for her life. The last thing she needed to be doing was wandering the woods at night.

Carrie wasn't sure what to do. She'd promised Brett that she would wait for him to get help. But she'd been in a haze and wasn't sure how long she'd been out of it.

A quick glance at her watch indicated that it had lasted a good half hour.

Shit! I've been out of it for a half hour? Crap.

A part of Carrie's senses was telling her to remain in one place. That way, she could wait for Brett; they could go get help together and then return to find Roy and Anita. But another little voice inside her mind was urging her to take action.

She's sick, possibly dying. You can't leave her out there to wander through the wilderness on her own! What kind of person would that make you? You're just scared about seeing that hag again, aren't you? Stop being such a scaredy-cat and do the right thing.

Carrie knew that her hesitation to venture outside was most definitely tied to the fear that she might see the crazy old woman again. The memory of the face in the mirror was quite vivid, and she could still see the drooling, evil mouth grin at her. It was the most frightening thing she'd ever seen and the idea that she could possibly come face-to-face with it again left her nearly paralyzed.

Taking a deep breath, she concluded that if Anita died in the woods tonight because no one had helped her—that would be the biggest horror of them all.

The answer was clear.

Go out, and be brave.

Carrie went over to the kitchen and picked up their last remaining flashlight. She was relieved to see that there was only one left, which meant that at least Anita had taken the one by the front door before venturing out into the woods.

Still, the idea of the sick woman maneuvering through the trees and brush was unnerving. Carrie pushed the thought out of her mind, and made her way through the trees into the darkness.

Everything hurt, but Anita chose to continue moving forward. She could see flaps of skin hanging off of her legs as she put each foot in front of the other one. Her entire body now felt like it was on fire, and ooze continued to drip as she fought to maintain her progress.

Her plan was simple: follow the dirt path until it dead-ended at the front of the park. She remembered that it had led them in a relatively straight line to their cabin, so she was confident— or as confident as she could be, given the circumstances—that if she continued onward, eventually she would end up at the entrance.

And eventually to a hospital, she thought.

It never occurred to Anita that she was being strong and incredibly brave, particularly given the fact that she was intensely afraid of illness and was now suffering from one of the worst sorts of bacterial infection possible. In general, she considered herself somewhat of a survivor and found that it was her very nature that kept her moving forward.

But shadows of doubt were casting themselves in her mind. The condition she was in was worsening, and she didn't have to be a doctor to understand that her time might be running out.

In fact, she was beginning to experience different types of pain that extended beyond her flesh. Breathing was becoming increasingly difficult, and she could hear the rattling of each breath as pushed forward through the woods. The exertion was making her head hurt as well, and Anita could feel a strong headache begin to take shape. Overall, she felt sick and weak and … faint. The sensation was scary and unique in its intensity, but adrenaline was keeping her from completely passing out.

As she walked along, Anita thought about Roy. He'd been gone for hours, and she wondered what had happened to him.

One thing's for sure. If I survive this crazy night, I'm definitely breaking up with him. He's a worthless asshole for leaving me all night to deal with this shit. He'd better be standing several yards away when I see him, or I'm gonna deck him so hard his head will spin.

The thought was funny, but Anita barely cracked a grin. She just put her head down and kept walking.

After a few minutes she could see the moon's reflection off the lake that she and Roy had visited earlier. In the dead of night, the lake looked quiet and mysterious, with barely a ripple moving along the surface.

Anita was thirsty. Her throat was parched, so she decided to make a quick detour by the water's edge and get something to drink.

And hopefully avoid the damned log that had gotten her so sick in the first place.

Fucking nature, she thought as she neared the water.

The dirt that ran along this part of the park seemed softer, and Anita noticed that her shoes seemed to sink as she approached the crystalline surface of the lake. It hurt her to walk on this type of terrain, as it required more strength to lift up each leg as she pushed forward.

"Oww," she moaned. It was difficult moving through the muck, and each leg lift once again revealed skin that was flapping in the wind and falling off.

"One more inch," she said out loud to no one in particular. Her whole world was pain now, so speaking to herself was just another way to survive the minutes of agony.

Finally, she reached the water's edge. Without thinking or even considering how filthy the lake might be, she cupped her aching hands and put them in the water.

She instantly pulled them out, because as soon as her hands had connected with the liquid, she'd felt a searing pain. The water felt like acid connecting to her skin and tears popped into the corners of each eye as Anita struggled to hold it together.

"Fine, I'll just kneel down and drink," she said in a tearful whisper.

Slowly dropping to her knees, the sick woman strained against the pain that shot through every limb and muscle. Shaking, she lowered her head to the surface of the lake and sucked in the cool water.

As she drank her throat hurt like madness, but the water did give her some relief from thirst, and she felt a tiny bit better.

When she was done drinking, Anita closed her eyes, afraid that she might catch sight of her deteriorating countenance, and slowly rose to a standing position once more. Her feet had sunken into the ground quite a bit and the dirt was up to her ankles, but the soothing, cool feeling of the dirt was providing a bit of comfort against her wounds, so she remained in place.

Then she heard it.

It was a whisper that was hard to identify at first. Anita couldn't tell if it was male or female or if she'd even actually heard something. But it was enough to make her stop and listen.

Then she heard it again. The sound traveled towards her as a warm wind blew over the lake, and it sounded like someone was whispering her name. Anita wondered if her mind was playing tricks on her and she was hearing things because of her growing illness. But instead of continuing on the path she remained in place, hoping to hear the sound again.

Anita … Look over here.

Now, Anita could clearly hear the voice, and she looked out over the lake. She could have sworn the voice was calling out to her from the other side of the medium-sized body of water, but everything looked relatively still and calm.

"Is someone out there?" she called in a shaky voice. She felt strange shouting across the lake in the middle of the night, but felt certain that someone on the other side was trying to get her attention.

Then, she saw Roy. He was in the center of the lake, his head and shoulders peeking out above the water. Anita wasn't sure why she hadn't noticed him before.

Anger coursed through her veins, and tears immediately

start to fall down her cheeks. Anita couldn't believe that after everything she'd been through, he was in the damned lake acting like everything was fine.

That asshole, she thought. *He's having a fucking vacation, and I'm in serious trouble. Doesn't he see how sick I am?*

"What the hell are you doing out there?"

Roy didn't answer and ducked his head under the water.

Anita was furious and prepared herself for what she'd say when they came face-to-face. Standing firmly, despite her deteriorating health, she managed to put her hands on her hips and waited.

Within a few seconds, Roy emerged again. He was closer, and she could see his face more clearly.

And when she did, her heart began to race.

Something was wrong with him.

Roy's skin looked almost gray against the night sky, and there were deep circles under his eyes. He stared at her—expressionless.

"Aren't you going to say something?"

He didn't flinch, but just then—a breeze swept through and with it, his response.

"You're going to die out here. You're going to die."

The last word spoken was louder in volume than the rest and cut through Anita's ears like a carving knife.

Without responding, she turned and tried to run. But her feet were entrenched in the mud, and she had to focus on pulling her legs out.

It hurt like hell.

"Ouch!" she screamed and tugged, desperate to get away.

She could hear splashing in the water behind her and knew that whatever Roy had turned into, it would be upon her faster than a New York minute if she didn't get her feet out of the mud.

Come on, come on, she begged, praying that she could get her shoes out of the muck. Finally, she decided it would be better to run on her sore feet than end up with Roy. She quickly wiggled her feet out of the flip-flops, turned, and ran.

The rocks and branches tore at her soles, but Anita no longer cared. She fled as if she was running on silk and tried to block out the whispers that followed her.

CHAPTER 10

Brett stared at the dusty portrait in his hand, trying to make sense of it. The image was definitely Jack Blaze, but he couldn't understand why it was engraved with the year 1989. The man in the photograph looked identical to the park ranger they'd seen earlier in the day, but more than twenty years had passed.

So how could he still look the same today as he did twenty years ago?

Maybe you saw a ghost, a small voice whispered to him.

Brett shook his head. He didn't believe that ghosts existed. If anything, he'd seen someone who was similar in features, but even still, why was the building in such disrepair? They'd been standing outside earlier in the day and yes, they'd been tired from the drive, but wouldn't they have noticed that they were standing next to a building that had been condemned?

None of it made any sense at all.

And what about the woman he'd seen? She looked awful and was obviously sick, but why hadn't Jack told them that there were guests staying in one of the nearby cabins?

Had they been fooled?

Yep, you always get what you pay for.

Sighing, Brett realized that there was no help coming and they were on their own. He considered checking the last room and then decided to pass on the idea. The shuffling noise he'd heard was probably the paper on the ground moving around, and he didn't have time to keep investigating.

Anita was too sick, Roy was missing, and he'd left Carrie to deal with everything back at the cabin.

Some date I took her on, he thought. *I'll be lucky if she ever speaks to me again after this debacle.*

He exited the building and once outside, immediately looked for his car. To his relief, the vehicle was still parked in the same spot.

But there was a problem.

The park gates were closed.

He walked over and examined the long arms. To his surprise they looked extremely rusty close up, and he tried to remember if the metal had seemed as worn when they'd first driven up. He couldn't recall, but as he ran his fingers gently along the metal, pieces of old paint flicked off into his hand and tumbled to the ground.

Brett examined the junction of the two arms and was distressed to find that they were indeed locked by a large padlock. He yanked on it fruitlessly to see if perhaps it wasn't locked, but was unable to manipulate it.

I wonder if there's a key.

Brett tuned the lock over and shined his light on the metal. A large keyhole gaped back at him, almost seeming to mock his circumstance. He considered going back to the office to search for a key, but decided the best thing to do was to bring Carrie and Anita to the office. He figured it might take him a while to find the key on his own and if he had help, they might uncover it faster. He also didn't want to leave them alone for too long, and if worse came to worst, they could hop the gates and start walking to safety, even though they were miles away from anything. They might still be able to flag down a car and ask for help once they got back to the main highway.

But that would mean trekking down that awful road in the middle of the mountain. Shit.

The uneven terrain with the cliffs on each side would be difficult to navigate in the dark, and Brett wasn't sure Anita could make the journey, which would mean having to leave her behind. Another unfavorable solution.

Sighing, he turned and before he even realized he was doing it, Brett began heading back towards the woods. He felt a bit lost but knew that there was nothing else he could do.

He started following the trail and had been walking for nearly five minutes when he heard a male voice. Surprised to be in the presence of other people, Brett looked around wildly, hoping it was someone who could help him. But the woods seemed dark and empty.

Brett was about to take a few more steps, when he saw a yellowish light in the distance. He could also hear several voices in discussion.

Heart racing, he quickly ran toward the light. Tree branches scratched and bit at his face, but Brett pushed them aside as he fought to make his way toward the glow. He powered through the trees like a marathon runner completing a long race and then stopped.

It was evident where the light had come from: a group of people had gathered in the dark and were holding flashlights to help guide their way. A man stood in the center of the group and was talking in a low, animated voice.

Brett recognized him almost immediately.

It was Park Ranger Jack Blaze.

As in his portrait in the office, the park ranger was sporting a full beard and seemed a bit heavier than he had earlier in the day.

"Ranger Blaze, is that you?" Brett asked, winded from the exertion.

But Jack did not answer and instead turned to the group that was around him and continued the discussion.

"Ok, what's done is done. She had to go. Now we've all gotta go back to our lives and forget this ever happened."

"But how do we forget?" one woman asked. "Did ya see her? She was laughing all the way down."

"Yeah, she's evil," another man said.

"Yes, she was evil. But now she's gone. Killing the bitch was for the best. We've got the children to think about."

The group murmured in agreement and started walking back toward the woods.

"Wait!" Brett called out. "Who are you people? Can you help me?"

No one responded, and Brett was shocked to see that the

people disappeared as they walked away.

Disappeared into thin air …

He stood for a moment; feeling like someone would come around the corner and tell him that what he'd seen was a big joke. But the next voice he heard wasn't a friendly one, and it sent chills running up and down his spine.

"They thought they got the best of me, eh?"

Brett turned to find himself standing very close to the woman from the cabin.

She looked old and worn, her eyes completely black and spittle dripping from her mouth with very word she formed.

He instinctively backed away and felt adrenaline begin to pump into his veins as panic slowly began to set in.

"Yeah, you look scared shitless," she said. "And ya should be. Them people thought you could end 'ol Sandy's life and git away with it. Well, I showed them. And if ya know what's good fer ya, it might be best to leave this place."

Brett nodded dumbly and watched as the hag turned and disappeared into the trees, leaving him alone in his terror.

Then he heard another sound. It sounded like someone dragging their feet through the woods and wheezing loudly.

He shined his flashlight in the direction of the shuffling and could barely make out a figure approaching.

"Hey, who's there?" he called out. All of his nerves were on edge, and he prepared himself for the worst.

A bout of coughing responded, followed by a weak voice. "Anita. It's Anita."

Brett ran over to the woman, who was hunched over and slowly dragging herself forward. He immediately recoiled and had to force himself to not reveal his true expression.

She looked like a zombie. Pieces of skin were hanging off her legs like shorn strips, her entire face was red and bloody, and her clothes were soaked and dark.

It was amazing to him that Anita was still walking, given her condition. He approached her cautiously as she stood in place, swaying back and forth.

"Anita, how did you get here? Are you ok?"

She lifted her head and even in her sick condition, managed

to give him a wry smile. "Do I look ok?"

Her words were interrupted by a bout of coughing. When she was done, she managed to choke out, "I walked here. Left Carrie at the cabin because she was acting weird. I saw Roy. He's not right. Something's wrong with him!"

She started sobbing and crumpled to the ground in a fluid heap.

Brett knelt down and took her gently by the shoulders. He winced as his hands touched the fabric, which was moist with ooze. "What do you mean you saw Roy?"

Anita looked up at him, her tears shining in the moonlight, "I saw him in the lake. He didn't look normal. Something's happened to him. Brett, we've got to get out of here."

He nodded and looked beyond Anita at the darkened woods. The last thing he wanted to do was venture back toward the cabin, but Carrie was still inside and he couldn't just leave her there.

First though, Anita needed to be tended to.

"Ok," he said with as much confidence as he could muster. "We've got to get you back to my car. Then, I'll go back and find Carrie."

"Need … a hospital," Anita whispered. Now that she'd found Brett, she was losing energy fast, and the world seemed to be swimming in and out of focus.

"Yeah, we'll get you to a hospital as soon as we get out of here. You've gotta help me, though, and stand up. Then just lean on me, like this. Ok?"

Anita stood up shakily and with Brett's help, managed to lean on him as they stumbled back to the office building at the front of the park. As the building slowly came into view, she hesitated and then stopped.

Brett looked at her questioningly. "What's wrong?"

"It's the building. It looks … weird. What's wrong with it? Why does it look so different now?"

"I noticed the same thing. It looks old now, like it's about to be torn down. Not sure what's going on. You're not going in there."

Anita didn't respond and just allowed Brett to lead her over to his car.

When they got to the vehicle, he struck his forehead in exasperation.

"Holy fuck. I totally forgot my keys in the cabin. That's just great. Do you think you can sit here and wait for me?"

Anita nodded.

Brett was about to head back into the woods when he turned back. "Hey, you said Carrie was acting weird. What was she doing?"

"She was kinda out of it. Was just sitting there and staring off into space. Like on a crazy drug trip or something."

"Really? Carrie's normally not like that."

Anita didn't respond and just sat on the ground, propping up her back against the tires. As soon as she leaned back, she closed her eyes.

Damn, this really isn't good, Brett thought.

He turned around and headed back into the woods, all of his thoughts now focused on getting Carrie, finding Roy, and getting the hell out of there.

Carrie's flashlight was starting to go dim. She shook it several times, which seemed to help momentarily, but then the light would start wavering again. To make matters worse, she wasn't sure if she was following the right path, because she'd just started walking in a general direction without looking at the ground and only noticed that she might be off course when leaves started crunching under her shoes.

Fuck! The ground beneath me is supposed to be smooth. When did I venture off course?

Her heart started racing at the thought that she might be lost. It was incredibly dark, and from what she'd seen during the daytime, the park was expansive. She knew that it was possible to get lost for hours, maybe even days if a person strayed too far from the main path.

Suddenly, the snapping of a branch caught her attention. She stopped walking and waved her flashlight in different directions.

"Hello?" she called out. "Is anyone there?"

The sound of another branch snapping was the only reply.

Carrie could feel beads of perspiration starting to form on her forehead and decided that instead of standing still and talking to the darkness, it might be best to keep moving. She began walking again, and increased the pace of each stride so that she was speed walking.

The snapping and crackling sounds seemed to be increasing from behind her, so she picked up her pace to the point where she was now quickly jogging through the woods, trying to avoid some of the branches that were hanging lower and blocking her path.

Carrie ... Carrie ...

She could hear her name being whispered as a warm wind blew through the trees and past her face. The voice calling out to her was breathless and it seemed as if the wind was speaking to her.

Or maybe I'm just losing my freaking mind.

Carrie started to run and was now fleeing through the woods. The trees and shrubbery passed her on each side in a blur, and she was barely aware of the fact that her flashlight went out when she ran straight into a solid wall.

Only when she stopped, she realized that it wasn't a solid wall after all.

It was Roy.

"Oh my God, Roy!" she screamed in relief. "I'm so glad that I finally found you!"

Carrie put her arms around his shoulders and hugged him tightly, but when she did, she noticed that Roy's skin was cold and soft.

She backed away slowly and looked at him carefully. "Roy, are you ok? Where have you been?"

He looked strange to her. His face was pale and there were deep circles under his eyes. He wasn't wearing a shirt or shorts and stood in front of her in his underwear.

Carrie could see that he was well endowed, the outline of his penis clearly apparent as his briefs were entirely soaked. He looked as if he'd been sitting in a pool of water and just emerged.

"You're totally wet and practically naked! Are you ok?"

Roy still didn't verbally answer, but nodded his head slowly.

It occurred to Carrie that the man might be in shock and had possibly been wandering the woods for hours in his underwear, looking for their cabin. A wave of sympathy washed over her, and she carefully took his hand.

"Look, let's go find Brett and then we can get you into some dry clothes. Ok?"

Roy nodded again, and they began walking together.

"So I'm glad we finally found you. Anita isn't doing well. She's got some sort of nasty bacterial infection and her whole body is reacting to it. It's pretty bad, so we've gotta get her to the hospital as soon as possible."

There was no response from Roy, who continued staring straight ahead.

"I know you guys haven't been getting along lately, but she really needs you right now. It's serious, Roy. You've gotta be there for her. She's really sick. Do you understand?"

There was still no response and Carrie was beginning to get irritated. She knew that he might be dealing with some emotional trauma over getting lost and being stuck out in the woods most of the night, but he needed to pull it together. They were all in this nightmare. Didn't he realize that?

She stopped walking and grabbed Roy's shoulders, turning him to face her.

"I don't know what's—"

Her words were cut off as Roy grabbed her around the waist and pulled her tightly against his body.

She could feel the bulge in his wet briefs press against her as he brought his face down to hers and kissed her lips. His mouth felt cold, but for some reason, her body was responding to the feel of his sex against her crotch. His penis felt warm and that warmth radiated through the fabric of her shorts straight through to her own sexual spot.

A moan escaped her lips as she writhed against Roy's body, feeling sweet sensations begin to throb between her legs. She pushed against him and inhaled his scent …

… which smelled like rot.

"What the hell?" She gasped as she backed away.

Roy looked at her with an amused grin, his erection clearly

visible against the stark white briefs. He opened his mouth and dark worms began falling to the ground in succession, landing in a pile at his feet. Their fat bodies then began wiggling out of his nostrils and even his ears became dark with pulsing, wet vermin.

Carrie backed away in shock. Her body threatened to shut down altogether, but there was a small voice in the back of her mind screaming for her to run away. She opened her mouth and tried to say something, but her tongue felt as if it was frozen to the top of her mouth.

She heard someone whisper her name again.

Carrie ... Carrie

This time her legs were listening and managed to carry her in the other direction and away from the creature that was once Roy.

Even with her eyes closed, Anita could tell that Brett had left. She could hear the crackling of the grass as he shuffled back into the forest. When the sound of his footsteps faded into the distance, the silence of the night once again crept in to fill the empty space, leaving her keenly aware of how alone she was.

Alone and vulnerable.

It hurt to move, but Anita felt the need to open her eyes and look around. When her gaze rested upon the building that Ranger Jack Blaze had occupied, her mind swirled with questions.

Why does it look so rundown?

And where is the door? I don't remember seeing an open space like that. It was only nine or ten hours ago that we were standing there, so why does it look so old?

Then, something caught her attention.

It was a round orb of light that appeared to be hanging in the center of the gaping darkness of the entrance.

"What is that?" she asked out loud.

The orb bobbed up and down for a moment and then disappeared.

Despite her illness and growing urgency for medical care, Anita's curiosity burned painfully. Every fiber in her body told her that it was important to follow the light, even if it might lead to mortal danger.

So, grunting loudly, she managed to pull herself up into a standing position. She watched in horror as more skin simply slithered down her legs and fell to the ground in a grotesque heap. As the dermis detached, rivers of agony flooded her thoughts and threatened to shut down her mind completely.

If you pass out now, you may never wake up, a small voice chided her angrily.

"Ok," she said with as much confidence as possible and to no one in particular. "I'm going to find out what that light was. And damn it, I'm not going to die out here!"

After some effort, Anita was able to stand in an upright position. Hands clenched into painful fists, she slowly made her way to the building, one foot at a time. Each step sent electric anguish up through her heels into her aching bones.

It took several minutes, but she finally made it to the building's entrance. Her eyes drank in the dusty air that swirled in the center of the doorway. Cracks hugged the jagged, rotting wood, and small weeds peeked out from the different lines that ran vertically and horizontally along the face of the structure.

The building looked abandoned, but Anita couldn't figure out how that was possible. When they'd seen it earlier, it had appeared clean and relatively new.

"Jack Blaze?" she called out.

A whispered chuckle responded.

Stunned, she backed up and felt adrenaline begin to kick in.

"Hello? Is someone there?" she called out.

As if in response, a warm wind shot out from the entranceway and traveled around her face, encircling her body and exiting to the parking lot. The wind smelled old and musty—filled with dust and filth.

Taking a deep breath and against her better judgment, Anita decided to go inside. She stepped over the threshold and could feel her feet slapping against the concrete floor.

Then she saw the round light again. It was flat against the wall at the back of the structure and was wobbling a bit. It looked as if someone was holding a flashlight straight ahead and turning the face of the light slowly to make little circles against the concrete. Anita turned around quickly, but there was no one behind her.

She couldn't figure out where the light was coming from, but something about it was attracting her ... pulling her forward as if by an invisible magnet.

Anita began to move toward it, and the closer she got, the dimmer the light became. By the time she was standing directly in front of the wall, the light had transitioned into a dim, fuzzy glow.

She reached out and tried to touch it, feeling the cold concrete beneath her bleeding fingers as they gently stroked the wall, leaving trails of ooze in their path.

Then, the light moved to the right and disappeared into a room.

Anita hesitated. Given the circumstances, she wasn't sure she wanted to venture forward. In addition, she'd mistakenly left her flashlight on the ground by the car because she'd been so mesmerized by the glowing orb.

As she moved to get a better look, her jumbled nerves dissipated a bit when she discovered that this particular room had a window that was letting in some moonlight.

Good. That should help me walk around so that I don't end up tripping or stepping on something that causes more damage to my broken body.

Carefully, she stepped inside and looked around.

The orb had disappeared, but the moonlight was casting a bluish glow on the contents that lay within the room, giving her an eyeful.

There were boxes stacked up against one of the walls in rows of five, and each grouping was labeled differently. In the center of the room, there was a small working table that was surrounded by chairs and covered with different papers. In the corner, a roll of "No Trespassing" tape lay on its side.

Anita walked over to the table and noticed a manila folder that had the word "Clippings" written on the tab in bold black letters. Feeling slightly lightheaded, she decided to sit down and take a minute to catch her breath. But in her ailing condition, it wasn't easy to navigate into a different position, and the sick woman cried out in pain as she slowly lowered herself onto one of the metal foldout chairs. Once she was able to fully rest her weight on the seat, Anita reached out and pulled the folder closer, opening it.

Inside she found a variety of newspaper clippings, cut out into different shapes and sizes. Anita couldn't tell what year they'd been printed because the clippings had already been pulled from their respective papers, so she decided to read them and try to figure out what she was looking at.

The first one was short and relatively vague. It was a community notice that had been posted near a series of local advertisements:

"Notice: The Acre Oaks Park has been closed until further notice due to the recent discovery of dead animals and the tragic death of Ms. Sandra Nunkes. Trespassers will be prosecuted to the fullest extent of the law. Please observe this notice. The park will re-open within the next few weeks once all investigations are complete."

The next clipping she picked up was a news brief:

"Pine Mountain officials have re-opened Sunken Park (formerly Acre Oaks).

In an effort to increase the safety of its visitors, park officials will mark any visible mud pits with No Trespassing signs and will provide safety information to each guest.

Some local residents are angry that the park name has been changed and say it's an insult to the woman who died there. Others are complaining that county efforts to house local people in nearby cabins have been thwarted as the park formally takes over all of the structures and uses them for overnight guests.

Displaced residents have been given homes in the nearby Millentown community.

Park officials were unavailable for comment at press time."

Anita put the clipping on the table and picked up the next one.

"Police are still searching for the intruder who strangled a Pine Mountain woman to death. Marie Conners, who lived in the Acre Oaks community, was found Wednesday morning by her six-year-old daughter. Conners had been strangled by an unknown assailant while sleeping in her bed. Authorities are searching for a suspect, but are working with very few clues, as there was no forced entry into the home and fingerprints were not found at the scene. Anyone with information regarding this case should call Crimestoppers at 555-425-1957."

Anita didn't want to continue reading, but forced herself to look at the next clipping.

"Authorities answered questions today at a press conference regarding the recent rash of violence that has overtaken a small Pine Mountain community.

In April, local resident Sandra Nunkes died accidentally when she fell into a nearby mud pit by her home near Acre Oaks Park. Subsequently, local authorities closed the park and despite some criticism recently reopened it under the new name of "Sunken Park". Park officials committed to having better security to protect visitors from Mother Nature's hazards and cabin residents were relocated to homes in a nearby town.

Within the span of the past few weeks, there have been additional deaths occurring within the Acre Oaks community— with prominent Sunken Park Ranger Mr. Jack Blaze passing away two days ago after an apparent suicide.

Residents of the small community are demanding answers, but authorities aren't providing much information as there are few leads given the sterility of the crime scenes. In all instances, authorities have been unable to locate fingerprints or other clues to lead them to a culprit.

In an attempt to stem any further violence, authorities have closed Sunken Park until further notice. Acre Oaks residents have been advised to observe a mandatory curfew of eight o'clock and ensure that their home security systems are up-to-date.

If you have any information regarding any of the recent crimes committed in the Acre Oaks area, please contact Crimestoppers at 555-425-1957."

The other clippings were photographs of the victims. One was a grainy image of officials taking a body out of a house on a stretcher. The body was covered with a white sheet that was had dark blood spots in the center.

Anita dropped the papers back into the folder and stared at the wall. Then she lowered her head and began sobbing uncontrollably.

CHAPTER 11

B rett was now becoming more familiar with the park and was able to easily find his way along the trail. As he passed the other cabin in the distance, he did his best to ignore it entirely. But curiosity won over, and he glanced over his shoulder at the window that peered at him from the distance.

It was dark.

A shiver passed through his body, but he wasn't about to make the same mistake again and start snooping around. He was now aware that something horrible happened to Sandra Nunkes and wondered if there were people within the park who wanted to harm him and his friends.. The group of people he'd seen earlier had confirmed that all was not as it seemed, and if he wanted to see another day he needed to focus on getting out and not getting sidetracked further.

And they weren't all going to escape harm.

Anita had been hysterical, but he knew from her broken description that Roy was gone. Whatever had happened had been horrible, and there was no saving him. Brett knew that he would feel grief over the loss of his friend at a later time, but was unable to feel anything at the moment other than the urgency of escape. He picked up the pace and was finally standing at the front of their cabin.

Cabin C.

To his disappointment and concern, the door was wide open. He cautiously stepped inside and looked around. Carrie was nowhere to be found, so he grabbed his keys and other personal belongings, stuffing them inside his shorts pocket.

All of the flashlights were gone, but Carrie had accidentally left her purse in their room. He wondered if she'd left in a hurry.

Brett made sure to grab her wallet and dorm room keys, but as his fingers connected with the bedside table, he noticed something else.

The table was incredibly dusty. As if it hadn't been cleaned for months—maybe years.

As he looked around, Brett realized that the room looked dusty everywhere, and the bedspreads themselves appeared shabby and disheveled. Running his fingers through his hair, he tried to remember if the room had looked unkempt when they'd arrived earlier in the day and couldn't seem to recall.

Certainly if it had looked that dirty they would have noticed and complained.

But that was before everything started falling apart. Where are we really? he wondered. *Is it Sunken Park? Or some kind of Hell that we stumbled into?*

Brett wasn't a religious person, but found himself saying a prayer inside his head.

Please, God. Please let us escape from this horrible place and find our way out. I'm too young to die. It can't all end up this way. I haven't even gotten married yet or had a kid or made my way in this world and seen my career take off. I can't leave my mom and dad or my sister behind. Please don't let this be the end.

To his dismay, a tear spilled out of one eye and traveled down his cheek. Brett wiped it away and took a deep breath, trying to stay as calm as possible. He knew that he had to find Carrie and get her and Anita out of the park. But there were so many obstacles like finding a way to get the gates to open and driving in the dark through the terrible entrance road that wound through the trees.

It all seemed so overwhelming. In addition, exhaustion was beginning to set in and Brett could feel his remaining pillar of strength crack as the burden of their nightmare rested squarely on his shoulders.

I can't fall apart. I've got to keep moving.

To help focus his concentration, Brett grabbed a diet soda from the refrigerator but he couldn't help noticing that the appliance was no longer running. It was off, and dust had gathered in each corner and shelf.

He knew that something was happening. The park was changing, and everything that they'd seen or heard earlier had been an illusion. It was like a fairy tale that was slowly turning sour.

Flipping the top off, Brett tilted the can and drank the soda in a quick series of gulps. Thankfully it was still cool, and the caffeine quickly traveled through his system, providing him with an extra jolt to keep his senses on alert. He tossed the can aside and stepped out into the night, in search of Carrie.

I can't lose my cool.

I need to think and be calm.

Don't panic.

Carrie was doing everything in her power to calm her racing heart and prevent her mind from completely spiraling out of control. But the vision of Roy standing in front of her while creatures wriggled from his nose and ears, continued to play itself in her mind over and over.

Somehow she knew that the man she'd been walking with wasn't Roy. It had looked like him, but there was something *evil* about him now. The happy-go-lucky person she'd begun to get to know … was gone.

And now she was once again alone in the woods.

But now somewhere out there was a crazy Roy lookalike.

And the hag.

Carrie hadn't forgotten about the woman she'd seen in the mirror.

Who is she? And why did she appear in front of me like that?

As she continued walking along, Carrie was relieved to see that a smooth pathway was a few feet away. She had actually come upon a point where it created a fork that either went straight or turned sharply to the west. So there were two options.

The decision was simple, because the westernmost point of where the path was leading was exactly in the same direction she'd just come from, and there was no telling whether or not the Roy-creature was still there waiting for her. Carrie chose to follow the path in the other direction and hoped that she was walking north, which would lead her back to the parking lot.

As her feet connected with the smooth dirt, the sensation gave her a strong feeling of hope, and she began walking more quickly—eventually breaking out into a jog.

Sweat traveled down her forehead as she struggled to stay on the path and away from the rogue nature that appeared at every step. Bushes scratched her legs, stones threatened her balance, and tree branches hung low to the ground, just waiting for her to trip over them.

Suddenly Carrie saw light up ahead. Her heat rate picked up considerably, but she forced herself to continue along the path and not veer in a slightly slanted direction towards it. As she approached the glow, it became clear that the light was coming from inside a cabin, shining through dusty windows.

She recognized the cabin as the one closest to theirs—the one they had passed on their way in. She was confused and stopped jogging as her mind tried to process what was happening.

How is this possible? If I'm looking at the cabin we saw when we came in, then I would have passed our cabin, wouldn't I? And I've been running in one direction for close to an hour. Is it possible that I'm running in circles? Why is there a light inside that place? Is someone staying there?

Carrie decided to investigate.

She crept along the trees and slowly made her way toward the structure. As she got closer to the cabin, Carrie began to smell something in the air.

It was the aroma of something cooking, but it wasn't entirely pleasant. It had an acrid sharpness, like meat that was broiling with too many spices. In addition, the air smelled slightly smoky so she had a feeling that whoever was staying in the cabin had lit some logs in the fireplace.

Maybe I can get some help. But I need to be careful. Need to be sure whoever's in there is friendly before I go barging in like a lunatic. Plus, I'm sure I look like a total disaster.

Carrie carefully maneuvered around the trees and tried to not trip on anything as she made her way to the side of the house. Dust and cobwebs attempted to attach to her clothing, and she slowly dusted herself off. Normally she would have been disgusted by the filth, but now it was a mere inconvenience in the greater scheme of things.

She peeked over the window frame and tried to see through the dusty film that was resting atop the glass.

Inside, she could see that her assumptions had been accurate. A fire was kindling amongst several large logs in the fireplace. There were an array of pots sitting on the stove and kitchenware rested atop the counters. Some of the lamps were lit and radiated a dull yellow light.

Carrie strained her eyes to see if she could make out anything further, but it was very hard to see past the kitchen into the other bedrooms. She also couldn't tell if there was anyone inside, but she had a feeling that there had to be, given all the activity.

Her mind whirled quickly as she stared into the window.

I don't understand. Where did these people come from? We definitely didn't seem them on the way in. Maybe they stumbled upon this place the way we did. If they've got a working smartphone or internet service, we can get some help.

"Not polite to trespass, dearie."

Carrie nearly wet her pants at the sound of an older woman's voice chiding her. She slowly turned around and prayed that she wasn't going to be staring at the same hag from the mirror.

To her relief, the woman standing in front of the cabin looked normal and human. She was wearing an old peasant dress with a sash around the middle and had her hair pulled back by a worn looking rag.

"Don't be afraid. Why don't ya come in for a bit?"

"Oh, I don't want to bother you. I'm just on my way out to meet my boyfriend. We're leaving tonight because our friend is very sick."

The older woman shook her head. "Tsk, tsk. These things happen out here. These woods? Well, they've got a mind of their own, don't they?"

Carrie wasn't sure how to answer. The woman seemed *off* somehow, but she didn't want to be rude so she smiled and replied, "Yeah, you could definitely say that. We've had nothing but bad luck since we got here. The brochure definitely didn't describe any of this."

The older woman seemed to darken at Carrie's mention of a brochure.

"You found a brochure about this here park?" she asked.

Carrie nodded and explained how they'd found the last brochure in a rack at a nearby restaurant and how they'd come as a group to have some rest and relaxation. She paused and decided not to share what had happened to Roy and decided to focus on the need to reach the outside world.

"You wouldn't happen to have a working phone or a computer we could use to send a quick email, would you?"

The woman smiled at Carrie. "Why don't you come inside? I'll see if I can help you git a hold of someone."

Do I really want to go in there? This woman seems so weird. She sounds uneducated and she's missing teeth and, oh God, what if I'm never able to find my way out? She may be my last hope.

Carrie nodded quietly and followed the woman inside the cabin.

Immediately, the darkness of night was replaced by warmth and light. Carrie was surprised at how homey the small cabin was inside. Different rugs covered the wooden floors, blankets rested atop the couches, and there were pictures of different nature scenes on the walls.

In fact, the cabin looked more like a home than a temporary vacation spot.

"How long have you been visiting Sunken Park?" Carrie asked as the woman disappeared into one of the bedrooms.

"Oh, I've been here a while. It's such a quiet, beautiful place, isn't it?"

"Yes, it definitely is," Carrie responded.

She continued to walk through the living area looking around at everything. Her eyes rested on a photograph that was situated above the fireplace. It was in a frame and was resting atop a small shelf. The reflection of the small flames from the fire below cast skinny orange fingers along the glass, making it difficult to see the picture inside, so Carrie picked it up and stared at it carefully.

The photograph was of a group of people and, to her surprise, Ranger Jack Blaze was one of them. The picture was strange in that none of the people were smiling. Rather, they stood in a semi-circle, almost glaring at the camera.

They looked angry.

The photograph made Carrie feel strange, so she put it back on the mantel. She could hear the woman bustling about in the bedroom, so she tried to keep herself busy and continued walking around.

Carrie noticed another photograph in a frame. This one was sitting beside the couch, so she sat down next to it and picked it up from the table. The comfort of sitting was overwhelming and Carrie closed her eyes for a minute and let out a whoosh of air from her lungs.

Finally, a chance to rest.

When she opened her eyes, she took a look at the photograph.

It was a photograph of the woman from the cabin. She was in the forest and was surrounded by small animals on all sides and appeared to be knee-deep in some sort of muck.

All the animals around her were dead.

Oh shit. What the hell?

Carrie stood up quickly and dropped the photograph on the couch.

"Um, I think I'm going to leave," Carrie called out. "Don't worry about me. I'll find another way to get in touch with people. Thanks for your hospitality."

She turned to leave when the sound of a woman crying carried over to her ears.

"Hey, are you ok?"

There was no response, but she could still hear the crying.

Fuck. I can't just leave her in there. What if something's wrong with her?

Even though she knew that it probably wasn't the right move and it would be best to run far away from the cabin and all of its strange artifacts, Carrie began walking toward the bedroom. She wasn't sure if she was consciously moving in the direction of the crying, because her feet seemed to have started operating on automatic. In essence, she felt as if something or someone was pulling her forward with a force that had powerfully taken over. The doorway to the bedroom grew closer and closer until she was standing in the center of the opening, looking in.

The woman who had invited her in was standing at the window, staring out at the woods. She was no longer crying but intently looking through the dusty glass. Without turning to face Carrie, she put her hand out and motioned for her to come closer. She then pointed to the woods as if there was something she wanted Carrie to see.

Carrie didn't speak and continued to allow the force to pull her forward. She walked slowly over to the woman, who remained stoic and then followed her gaze to the window.

At first, there was nothing to see. The blackness of night created a shroud that simply reflected their own images back at them. Carrie tried not to stare at the older woman's reflection and kept her gaze on her own mirrored image, noticing how fear was clearly evident in both of her eyes.

Then, the darkness disappeared and to Carrie's shock, she was staring out the window and could see a scene playing out in daylight …

There was a group of people standing together in the center of the woods. Carrie recognized them from the photograph. They were all looking carefully at a spot along the ground that appeared dark and unstable.

"You think she's gone?" one of them asked.

"Yeah. She's gone. Now we need to do what we talked about and get on with it. We can't look back. Getting rid of her was the best thing fer everyone. Let's move on. And y'all need to keep quiet. Got it?"

The rest of the group nodded quietly.

Carrie looked over at the strange woman, who was still staring straight ahead. She turned back to the window, and now the scene changed. It split into four different quadrants somehow as if Carrie was watching different TV screens that had been pushed together to form one large image.

In the upper right, she could see a woman cooking dinner. As she stirred broth in a large vat, a dark form appeared from behind her. The woman in the image flinched as if she felt something, but didn't turn around. A moment later, the dark image reached out with two shapeless arms and pushed the woman's head down into the steaming liquid, holding her there. The woman's arms flailed but her head didn't emerge.

In the upper left image, a man walked along the road. He was smoking a cigarette and slowly ambling on as if he'd been drinking too much. A car light appeared in the distance and grew closer and closer.

Carrie's chest tightened with the understanding of what would happen next …

The car came closer and the man finally realized that it was approaching so he moved away from the road and continued trudging forward on the grass. The car approached quickly, and, in one fluid move, swerved and hit the man from behind. The image blurred as the man flew forward, the look on his face full of terror and pain.

The lower quadrants demonstrated similar moments of death. One woman was attacked in her bed by a blur of violence, while another woman who was standing on a cliff fell to her death.

The images continued to play while Carrie watched, horrified. But an understanding began to form in her mind.

These people weren't simply killed. They did something terrible to deserve their fates. But what did they do? They spoke of getting rid of someone. Did they kill someone and end up suffering the consequences of their actions?

"There's always a price to pay, dearie."

Carrie turned to look at the woman, who was still staring out of the window. She seemed thoughtful and unaffected by the horrific images that were playing out in their reflection.

"Who were those people?"

"Ah. They were folks who don't understand what they don't understand. They were too blind or stupid to realize that there's more than meets the eye. And now they're dead."

She cackled to herself.

Carrie started to back away from the window.

"They killed you."

The woman remained in place, but Carrie could tell that she was smiling.

"What's death, really? Is it the rotting of yer corpse? If so, then yer friend Anita is dead already. Is it lack of knowledge of who you are and what you've done? Then yer friend Roy is long gone."

She turned to face Carrie, who felt the blood drain from her face.

"Or is it the lack of vanity, dearie? If so, then you'd better run. Because that's one way to look at things, eh?"

And then, the woman's face began to morph into the same horrific hag that Carrie had seen in the bathroom. The one that was so frightening that it had caused her to black out entirely.

But Carrie was ready, and instead of standing in place, watching the hag fully transform, she ran from the bedroom into the living room, noticing that now all the lights were off and it was dark and cold.

Like death.

Carrie threw the cabin door open and ran back into the woods.

As her footsteps echoed through the warm night, she could hear the woman's evil laughter carry through the trees, twist in the wind, and permeate everything that grew in the darkness.

CHAPTER 12

C *ome with us.*

Anita wasn't sure how long she'd been sitting at the table, newspaper clippings surrounding her like soldiers preparing for an attack. She'd been sobbing, which then turned into moans of anguish as the pain from her illness continued to take over. Everything felt wet and awful.

Even her teeth hurt.

But then she heard a strange voice, and in the brief second that it spoke to her, the pain had mysteriously disappeared. The respite had lasted for only a moment and then the pain returned once more.

"Hello?" she called out. "Is anyone there?"

Come with us.

She looked around wildly, trying to find the source of the voice but the room was empty, and she wasn't sure if it was just the sound of the wind. She knew that in her current state, hallucinations weren't entirely out of the question.

Hell, my body probably wants to hallucinate so that it can't feel pain anymore.

With all the effort she had left, she pushed herself into a standing position and grimaced when she saw that parts of skin remained on the table. She imagined her body was turning into an onion that was slowly shedding its layers.

Until there's nothing left.

Shuddering, she turned and began to walk back down the hallway to the exit. To her surprise there were people standing in the entranceway. They were holding flashlights and motioned for her to follow them.

"Thank goodness you're here," she called out. "I'm really sick. Can you help me? I need a hospital!"

The people nodded and backed away from the entrance, disappearing into the night.

"Wait!" she called out. "Don't leave me here!"

Anita managed to make her way down the hall and exited the building as quickly as she could. She could see the group of people up ahead, but they were walking back into the woods.

Damn. I've got to catch up to them or I'm screwed. No sense waiting here for Brett. Maybe they have a car on the other side of the gate and can get us out of here faster.

"Hold up! Wait!" she called out, but the group continued to move into the darkness of the trees.

Anita took a deep breath and tried to pull herself together. Every step hurt—particularly since she was barefoot—and struggling to breathe, but her hope was stronger than any of her aches and pains and pushed her forward. She limped slowly after them and felt her heart surge when one of the men turned around and motioned toward her—

Thank God—they're going to help me!

She wasn't thrilled about going back into the woods, but figured that perhaps there was another exit somewhere where they'd parked. The landscape was so vast that she presumed it was possible for there to be other roads out.

As she followed the group, she became irritated when they moved off the path. It was more difficult to follow them through trees and shrubs, particularly when the ground was so uneven. A few times she felt her ankles nearly buckle and twist, but miraculously Anita was able to maintain her balance while continuing to keep the group in sight.

After a few minutes, she realized that the ground she was walking on was beginning to turn upwards and had started a slow incline. It made following the people harder but she managed to keep up. As she walked after them, she was surprised to see that the trees has started to thin out and they were making their way to some sort of landing. She wasn't sure if it was the top of the mountain or mountain-like terrain that lead them to cliffs that jutted up and flattened out.

Could be a place where we can get to a road. This is definitely looking good. And not a moment too soon. I'm not sure I can walk any farther. There's pain everywhere, and I feel like I'm losing my mind.

As she walked after them, Anita strained to hear the group. It was strange that they weren't talking to each other, just moving along in silence. She figured that something bad must have happened to them too, and that was why they were leaving.

Anita's thoughts turned to her mother again. She felt panic seep into her thoughts and struggled to maintain an inner calm.

I'm not going to turn out like her. This sickness may be some serious shit, but I'll make it. Carrie said she's seen this before, and there's a treatment to cure me. Wait, did she say that? I can't remember. It doesn't matter. I'm going to get to people who can take care of me.

Talking to herself made Anita feel better because it helped her ignore the pain that was starting to come in stronger waves. She forced herself into a sort of hypnotic pace where she simply focused ahead at the group of people who were leading her out of the park.

Finally, the group stopped and stood with their backs to Anita.

When she finally caught her breath and was able to reach the top of the incline, her eyes widened at the sight.

They were standing at the top of a cliff that was large enough to allow many people the opportunity to stand and admire the surroundings.

Oh my God. Look at that. There's nothing for miles around us but trees. It's beautiful, but where are the roads? Where am I?

"Excuse me," she called out. "Thanks for helping me, but where are we? Can we get out of the park this way? I need a hospital."

The people finally turned to look at her in unison. They were mostly couples, all easily within middle-age range and all wearing the same blank expressions.

Even though it was dark, the moonlight was providing ample lighting and Anita recognized their faces. They seemed familiar to her and then, complete realization set in.

I've seen those people in the clippings. Those are the people from the clippings!

She took a step back, not sure what to do, but the ground was uneven and it caused her to stumble.

One of the men put his hand out and spoke calmly. "Don't worry, you're ok. Following us was the right thing to do."

It was at that moment that something in Anita's mind completely snapped. Her exhausted and destroyed body had sustained all it could, and she could no longer fight back. All elements of reality had become cloudy and unclear, leaving her to make decisions that she normally would have never considered. As the people drew closer, she stared at their concerned faces and even though she knew they couldn't possibly be alive, as she had seen obituary photos of many of them in the mass of clippings inside the park ranger's building, she no longer cared. They were concerned for her well-being and wanted to help her.

They were her only hope.

Anita watched as Ranger Jack Blaze stepped out of the group and approached her.

He no longer looked stoic, but rather sympathetic and sad, his dark eyes filled with remorse.

"Follow us," he said.

Anita allowed Jack to help her back to her feet and she walked along the landing with him, the others in the group following behind her. She could see the edge of the cliff approaching, and yet, she did not feel nervous or panicked. She simply followed Jack's lead, and when he stepped all the way to the edge, she did not question him.

"This is how it must be, Anita. You'll now understand why we acted the way we did. Now you'll be one of us."

And with that, he pulled her forward, and they both leapt into the darkness that waited below.

CHAPTER 13

Brett walked slowly through the woods, calling out for Carrie as he followed the path.

It was three o'clock in the morning. A time that was often referred to as the "witching hour."

Brett had never met anyone proclaiming to be a witch, but he was pretty certain that Sandra Nunkes fit the bill perfectly. Obviously a group of locals had been interested in getting rid of her, and from the looks of the strange woman, she was obviously into some kind of black magic. But was it enough to warrant her death? He didn't agree that simply being a person who believed in the occult made it okay to be persecuted and attacked. After all, there were many people who believed in that kind of thing; weren't there? And if those people had killed her, was that why she was hurting others who trod on this land? Was she forever going to make people suffer for the wrongs done to her?

The whole thing seemed outrageous and sick, but Brett couldn't rule out the possibility that Sandra Nunkes was indeed a witch who was hell-bent on revenge. It just made the situation that much worse and the need to escape even more desperate.

"Carrie! Are you out there?"

Suddenly he heard a branch crack, and then the sound of leaves crunching as Carrie came racing out of the darkness.

She was covered in grime and her tearstained face looked terrified. At the sight of him, she leapt on top of Brett and held on to him tightly. He could feel her entire body shivering as she clung to him, whimpering into his shoulder.

They stood in an embrace for a minute, when he finally pulled back slightly and looked at her.

She was a mess, dirty, her clothes ripped, and scratches lined her legs and arms.

"What happened to you? Are you ok?"

Carrie's eyes filled with tears as she recounted the past hours that they'd been apart. Her voice broke and wavered as she detailed the woman in the cabin and her experience with Roy.

Brett stood and listened, feeling a chill as Carrie described the woman in the cabin who'd shown her several images of people who'd been killed in different ways. She was about to go on further when Brett interrupted her.

"I know who that is," he said. "That's Sandra Nunkes. I think she was killed in this park by a group of people who were scared of her for some reason. They were afraid that she was going to hurt their children or animals or something. I'm not exactly sure why they had to kill her, but they obviously thought she was dangerous. I've seen her too."

Carrie's eyes widened. "Why didn't you tell me? How can we be seeing her if she's dead? Is she a ghost?"

"I don't know. Something happened here, Carrie. I think she was killed by this group of people and then something happened to them. Remember the park ranger we saw earlier?"

"Yeah, what about him?"

"I think he's dead. And I think he's one of the people who killed Sandra."

Carrie grabbed Brett's hand and squeezed it tightly. "We have to get out of here. We've got to get Anita and get out of here before we're all dead."

He nodded and wiped the sweat off of his forehead. Brett wasn't sure if it was the right time to tell Carrie that the gates were locked and they had no way out unless they planned to escape on foot. Judging from her fragile state, he decided it would be best to walk back to the park ranger's office and then search for the gate key together.

Holding her hand, he led Carrie back on to the path and they began walking to the front of the park.

Anita felt air rushing by both sides of her face as her body fell at an incredible speed. Understanding that the end was near, she said a final prayer and waited for the embrace of death. But then the most unexpected thing happened.

Her body stopped falling and floated down slowly until her feet connected with the softness of grass. When she opened her eyes, she was astonished to see that the sun was shining and she was standing amidst a mass of trees. All around her nature hummed with the sound of crickets and birds chirping from their elevated positions.

She was standing alone and felt surreal. The pain was gone, and when she looked at her arms and legs she was surprised to see that the sores and decay had disappeared. She looked and felt fine.

Is this Heaven? she thought.

"No, it's the past," a voice explained from behind her.

When she turned around, she was surprised to see Jack Blaze standing behind her. He was wearing the same clothes as the prior day—khakis and a wide-brimmed hat. The park ranger's expression was serious, but there was a softness to his eyes that Anita noted almost immediately.

"What are we doing here?" she asked.

Jack sighed and looked up at the nearby trees. "We're in a place that should help you understand what's goin' on. There's no time or urgency here. It's just a place where a memory's been captured so that you can find peace in your final moments."

His words were strange and chilling, but Anita was beginning to understand that her life was over. Perhaps this strange dimension would provide answers to the questions that had been burning in her mind.

"Yes," Jack said, as he read her thoughts once again. "You'll understand why Sunken Park is such an evil place."

He pronounced the words "Sunken Park" as if they were distasteful and frowned, gesturing for her to follow him through the woods. As he began to speak once more, Anita noticed that his words were more refined than in the past when he'd spoken in a Southern twang. In fact, his voice seemed to resonate through the air and not really come from his lips, but rather from the strange warm winds that would periodically blow through the trees.

"This park is a strange place. For starters, it's not entirely public property. In the early seventies, some of it was bought up by developers in New York and they decided that it would be a good place to start a small, private community. They built cabins in the middle of the woods and tried to sell them to rich folks. Problem was, no one was interested in a small cabin in the middle of nowhere. Most folks wanted to be somewhat closer to civilization." He chuckled. "People only want to be so close to nature. If they're too far away, it can be pretty isolating."

Anita nodded.

"Anyway, they couldn't sell the cabins to outsiders, and eventually the developers went out of business due to some bad deals and the cabins went up for auction. County officials felt that it would be best to help out the locals who needed a place to live and who didn't mind living all the way out in the middle of nowhere. That's when we met Sandy."

Jack was quiet for a moment and walked out of the woods into a clearing. He pointed through the trees and in the distance Anita could see a cabin. She recognized that it wasn't the one they'd stayed at, but rather the one they'd passed on the way in.

"Sandy was a single woman with no children who came out of lord-knows-what hole and showed up at the auction. The people of the county felt bad for her and agreed to sell her that cabin at a reduced price that probably cost no more than a few bags of groceries. The other cabins in the area were purchased by some families in the community who were in similar financial trouble. And I decided to buy one of the cabins because I've always enjoyed nature and worked at the nearby park."

"Wait," Anita interrupted. "So these cabins weren't a part of the park? Where does the park end and the private land start?"

"The lake is the dividing line," Jack explained. "It was sort of a way to ensure that the locals enjoying the public areas didn't bother the families living here."

Anita's mind started to spin.

So we weren't staying in some vacation cabin. We were staying in someone's home!

"Not exactly," Jack continued, seemingly able to read Anita's mind, "When Sandy and the other families moved into the cabins, things were quiet for a while, and everyone seemed to be respecting each other. But then the situation changed. Some kids from the nearby families started noticing that Sandy never left the house, and there was always a weird smell coming from her chimney. Then some kids found strange bones in the bushes by her tree, and then … the dogs started disappearing."

Jack then described how it had started with one dog, then another, and then cats started going missing. The pet owners were devastated and thought that there may be mountain lions taking the animals, so they started setting traps. But the traps didn't help, and animals continued to disappear.

"And then it happened," Jack said, taking a deep breath. "One of the Millers' kids was snooping around outside Sandy's cabin when he discovered that the door was open. He went inside and into her kitchen, and that's where he found them."

"Found them?"

"Dogs. Cats. Birds. Every kind of animal you can imagine. She'd skinned them and stretched them out on her counter. She was cooking the animals and eating them, then taking their fur and making rugs and blankets. Thankfully the kid got out of there quickly, but when he got home and told his parents, all hell broke loose."

"I can imagine," Anita murmured.

"The parents called authorities, who showed up and searched the house. But they couldn't identify any of the animals because everything was skinned or boiled. The worst thing was what they found in her bedroom."

"What did they find?"

Jack stopped walking and turned to face Anita. "They found hundreds of photographs she'd taken from her window of the different children who lived out here. The kids obviously didn't realize she was taking the pictures, but she must have been standing at her window all day, just snapping portraits of them. It was downright horrible."

"But wait," Anita said. "That doesn't mean anything. Maybe she was just lonely."

"Lonely?" Jack asked with an exasperated expression on his

face. "Or insane? The parents already saw what she'd done to the animals and they didn't want to take any chances with their children. That's why we did what we did."

"And what exactly did you do?" Anita asked, her eyes piercing into his.

"I know you think what we did was wrong. It's written all over your expression, young lady. But we did what we had to do."

And as the words were spoken, the sky darkened quickly and the temperature in the air dropped dramatically. Anita stood and watched as the scene of Sandra's death played out in front of her.

The group of parents appeared as if a hologram had been activated, and she watched as they pulled Sandra from her home and dragged her to the center of a small clearing. She should see that the ground was a different color and watched with horror as Sandra Nunkes cursed the crowd and sank into the ground, a strange smirk on her face.

When the woman was completely submerged, the sky changed colors again, turning a deep purple. The landscape also began to change and shift.

Anita could feel the ground beneath her feet begin to grow softer and more pliant. An uneasy feeling began in the pit of her stomach and started to spread throughout her body. She looked up at Jack, who simply stared back at her with a sad expression on his face.

"You're right. We were wrong. No matter what she did to those animals or those strange photos in her bedroom, we shouldn't have killed her. But the problem is, we figured it out too late. And by the time we realized our mistake, she was dead and we all started facing the consequences of her curse. Our group started dying off. One by one, people were killed in different ways, until finally I was the last one left."

Her feet were starting to sink into the ground, so Anita shifted and tried to find something firmer to stand on.

Jack was also beginning to sink into the ground, but he didn't seem to notice or care. "After everyone was dead and gone, I decided to move out of the park and rent a small apartment a few miles from here. But I still worked in the park and somehow, I found myself constantly coming back to the spot where we'd killed her. Even after authorities found her body, I still came back to the same spot."

The man was now knee-deep in the mud while Anita struggled to keep her footing above ground. But now their surroundings had become muddy and dark—there was nowhere else to go.

"I couldn't sleep, couldn't eat. Even when I was promoted to Park Ranger, there was no relief from the curse that Sandy had put on us. And then, one night, I couldn't take it anymore. I drove out here in the middle of the night and put a gun to my head. They found my body in the same spot where we'd killed that poor woman."

Anita was horrified and found herself sinking into the ground beside Jack. She twisted and turned, but there was nowhere to go. And the more she twisted and turned, the faster she sank. Her eyes widened in terror as Jack began to change in front of her.

His skin began to turn gray and broke apart in different places, revealing blackened muscle underneath. It continued to slowly pull back and grow taut against his skull until he resembled a living corpse. But even as his lips began to shrink away, Jack continued to speak.

"We tried to convince ourselves that we did the right thing. But it was murder. And now, this place is cursed. That brochure you found … it's the one we made right before they shut the park down completely. After Sandy died, all the families had to move out of here, and we tried to rent out the cabins to overnight guests. We even changed the name of the park to Sunken Park to try to make a new start and highlight the fact that there are natural areas where the ground acts like quicksand. Like we were sending out a warning or something, while trying to honor Sandy's memory by using the letters of her full name. We tried to hide what we'd done. But it was too late. This place is evil."

"Help!" Anita called out. "Somebody help me!"

What was once Ranger Jack Blaze finally went under and

disappeared into the darkness of filth and regret, leaving Anita by herself.

She could no longer raise her arms. They felt glued to her sides and the mud was coming up fast now, reaching her chin. As it pulled her down, she said a final prayer for her mother, for herself, and for her friends, who were still trapped inside the hell of Sunken Park.

CHAPTER 14

"We're almost there. I can see the entrance from here."

Carrie didn't respond, but Brett could tell that she was excited because she had picked up her pace significantly. It had been tough going because she was still in shock and was barely keeping up. He hoped that now, the once-energetic blonde would find some inner strength and be able to handle the news he was about to share.

"Carrie, there's something you need to know."

"What?" she asked, looking up at him, her unkempt hair hanging in her face.

"There's a slight problem with the gate."

"What do you mean 'a slight problem'?'"

"It's locked. And I don't have the key."

Carrie looked at him with tired eyes. "Can't you just drive through it? Like in the movies?"

"No, it would totally wreck the car. The arms are too thick. There's a lock that we can try to break open, or there may be a key. We've got to go check."

"What about Anita?"

"She's ok. I left her by the car, so hopefully she's still conscious. We've got to get her to a doctor."

Together they made their way down the hill and approached the building.

Carrie stopped and inhaled quickly. "This can't be right."

Brett remembered that Carrie hadn't seen the building since they'd first arrived at Sunken Park. The last time she'd seen it, it had looked normal and relatively new. But there was no time to start explaining. She knew enough of what was going on, and he worried that any time wasted could result in further harm to both of them.

"Let's just go inside and see if we can find a key or something to break open the gate. I'll explain the rest in a min—"

Carrie interrupted him. "Didn't you say Anita was sitting by your car?" She pointed to the lot that was empty with the exception of Brett's parked vehicle. "She's not there. Where the hell is she?"

"Damn it!" Brett exclaimed. "I feel like we keep playing this out over and over again. Why couldn't she just stay in one fucking place? This is ridiculous."

"Brett."

"Yeah?"

"We need to get out of here. We can't go looking for her. If she's turned into a psycho like Roy, it's too late anyway."

The realization cut into his moral compass like a searing razor, but he knew that Carrie was right. Survival had become the most important thing, and if they didn't get out of the park soon, they would both end up like their friends.

Or worse.

Brett looked at the building and then turned his gaze back to Carrie. "I think it would be best if we go in there together. Things in this park aren't exactly what they seem, and I'm afraid if we separate it could be dangerous."

"Yeah, I totally agree. Let's just find a way out of here."

Brett took Carrie's hand in his and did a quick survey of the doorway. He was relieved to find that nothing had changed. Dust swirled inside, and the same cracks remained along the wall.

"Ugh. It's totally gross in here."

Brett didn't reply and just led Carrie inside. He did a quick inventory of the building—a small waiting area and four rooms on opposite ends of a long hallway.

Just the way he remembered it.

Thankful that nothing had changed, he started down the hallway and turned into the first room. It was the same one he'd been in before—the one with the all the boxes and supplies.

"Let's open some of these up," he instructed. "If we can't

find the key, we might at least find something to help us break the padlock."

Together, they started pulling boxes off of different large piles. As each box came down, dust came with it, causing them to cough and sneeze from the onslaught.

"This is horrible," Carrie said after a particularly long sneezing fit.

"I know, but we've got to find something to help us cut through the padlock." Brett stopped and thought for a moment. "If you want to do something else, why don't you check the different drawers? There are desks in a couple of the rooms in here. Why don't you go across the hall to the room across from us or search through the desk in the front lobby?"

"I'm scared, Brett. Are you sure I'll be ok rummaging around here on my own?"

"Don't worry, I'm right here," he assured her. "And take your flashlight so you can see what you're doing."

Carrie nodded and started walking to the door. Before she got there, she turned around and gave him a small smile. "If we ever get out of here, I'd like to spend much more time together. You seem like one of the good guys."

Brett felt heat rise to his face at the compliment. He stood up and walked over to Carrie, grabbing her around the waist and giving her a deep kiss.

They embraced, feeling an invisible strength wrap them up in its powerful arms.

Brett whispered, "Just be safe. I can't lose you."

Carrie felt fear begin to re-enter her psyche as soon as she left Brett in the supply room.

The hallway was dark and dusty, and even though the structure wasn't a large one, the idea of being alone anywhere inside its four walls just felt *wrong* somehow.

Still, she knew that they needed to find a way out quickly and driving was the safest option. But they had to get the gates open first.

"There has to be a key here somewhere," she muttered to herself.

Carrie decided to start with the lobby desk and then work her way back through the hallway. Having worked in numerous front-desk jobs throughout college, she knew that most companies entrusted their keys to the receptionist, as that was the person who most employees were likely to go to for help—particularly people who accidentally got locked out of their offices and who was also typically the person letting maintenance and repair people into the building.

But this lobby was not like one of the places she'd worked in before. It was old, dusty, and downright disgusting.

This place is a dump. It looks like it's been vacant for years.

Carrie walked over to the desk and began looking for drawers. She felt a surge of hope when she identified a set of pullouts. She grabbed one of the handles and tried to open it.

The drawer was rusty and would only give halfway. It felt like there was something inside that was keeping it from opening all the way.

She took a deep breath, and, wrapping her fingers around the handle, tugged as hard as she could to pry it free.

The drawer screeched in protest but finally flew open, sending several folders into the air. They fluttered in the dusty wind and fell to the ground in a messy heap.

Carrie immediately ran her fingers through the drawer, hoping to connect with something metallic, which would indicate a key or scissors. But her searching was fruitless and revealed only a few pieces of paper and the smooth, sharp feel of a few pencils that were rolling around in the back of the enclosure.

"Damn."

The folders were lying at her feet, so she decided to pick one up. The tab on the folder had the word "Staff" printed on it.

Carrie placed the folder on the table and began to sift through the paperwork. The folder contained files that gave the background on the different people who worked at the park. And judging from the dates that were printed in the right hand corner of each page, the files were from the early to late eighties.

She did a quick once-over on some of the pages and stopped when she got to one particular piece of paper.

It was marked "Fred Windler."

Holy shit! That's my uncle.

Carrie's uncle Fred had been living in Atlanta for many years, but he was a recluse who worked as an accountant and spent very little time with the family. She'd only met him a few times in childhood, and her parents had always referred to him as someone who didn't feel the need to spend much time around others. He'd been married once and was now divorced with no children.

Feeling her heart start to race, Carrie began to read the file. It listed her uncle's age as nineteen and described his work history as a part-time summer job. As she looked through the details of his file, she noticed that one of the things he'd been responsible for were weekday visits to pick up any trash that the "residents" had left near the park.

Residents? She thought. *I guess at one time there were people living here.*

Carrie couldn't find anything else about Fred's work history, so she continued to flip through pages that contained information about the different teenage staff members who were all part-timers. Her hands trembled as she found names that seemed striking familiar ...

"Rick Duntman."

"Dewayne Johnson."

"Tina Davila."

The pages dropped from her hand and drifted slowly back down to the table. The world around her had started moving in slow motion, but Carrie didn't notice because her mind was in another place.

It all became clear.

They'd been lured here.

They were all ... connected.

"Oh no. What have we done?"

Carrie turned to warn Brett, but as she tried to shift her body, she realized that it was next to impossible. The air around her had gotten heavier somehow, and it felt like she was moving through quicksand.

And then, the world around her began to change.

The walls started to turn a brighter shade of white. The dust disappeared into thin air. The darkness was replaced by brightness, and, suddenly, what was night …

… turned to day.

Carrie watched as the world around her transformed like in a scene change during a movie. Amazingly, people appeared out of thin air and began to walk in and out of the building, sometimes passing through her immobile body as if she wasn't there.

As her eyes drank in the incredible phenomena that was occurring around her, she noticed that a group of teenagers had filed in the front door and were now standing in the lobby area together.

They looked nervous and kept snatching glances at each other as they stood and waited for something.

Carrie stared at the different faces and wasn't entirely surprised to see a younger version of her uncle Fred standing among the group. He looked worried and was holding the hand of a redheaded girl who rested her shoulder against his.

Someone else came into the room. Even with his back to Carrie, she immediately recognized him.

Park Ranger Jack Blaze.

"Thanks for coming in," he said. "I know some of you weren't supposed to work today, but we've got to discuss something very important. And what we're about to talk about can't leave this room. If anyone ever found out about this, you could all end up in jail. Do y'all understand?"

The teens nodded in unison.

Wow, Carrie thought. *They all look terrified.*

Those poor kids.

My poor uncle.

"It's come to my attention that y'all have been talking about the woman who's been missing for a few days. And I've heard that one of you found a few pieces of torn clothing on a log near the park's border. Am I right?"

One of the teens, a tall, lanky kid, nodded miserably.

"On top of it, I've heard that one of you has been messing with the mud pits that are on our property. Am I right?"

An African American teen of about fifteen who was standing with the group looked down at the floor miserably. Carrie knew immediately that he was related to Roy. His eyes and face were very familiar, and it was if she were staring at a slightly younger version of her friend.

"All right. Well, for starters, you're not fired."

An audible sigh of relief came from the group. They had clearly thought that they were getting the ax.

"But before y'all get comfortable, we need to make sure we're clear. None of you say anything about those strange piles of mud. Understand? Stay away from them. Don't talk about them. We'll take care of business. There's nothing there but a bunch of trash that we'll clean up later this week. Got it?"

The teenagers were silent for a moment.

"Do you understand?" Jack repeated. "We don't need a bunch or stupid teenagers spreading rumors about Sandy's disappearance. The lady's a nutcase and she probably ran off. But for your own safety, keep doing what you're hired to do. Understand?"

This time, the teenagers got the message loud and clear. They nodded in unison and filed out of the building together.

Carrie watched as the park ranger stood still, waiting for the lobby to empty out.

Once everyone was gone, he lost his steadfast composure and put a hand to his face.

"Damn," he whispered. "We need to get this shit under control."

Jack then turned and went back down the hallway, leaving Carrie by herself for a few minutes.

She waited and wondered if now, the world would go back to normal and allow her to find Brett. There was no doubt in her mind that they had stumbled into a nightmare and needed to run far away from the cursed park.

If it will let us. If she will let us. Good 'ol Sandra may not want to let us go. Who knows how long she's been cursing our families?

Carrie could hear Jack rustling some papers in the back of the building and then watched as he re-emerged carrying a big garbage bag. It was stuffed with trash and she could only imagine how many secrets he was taking to the dumpster. As he walked to the front door, she could tell that he was weighted down with not only the heavy bag, but also with the knowledge he carried with him.

As he neared the door, his exit was suddenly blocked by a couple of men who were casually dressed but wore serious expressions of their faces.

"Jack, have they found anything?" one of the men asked anxiously.

The park ranger shook his head and gestured towards the bag. "Nope. And they won't. I'm getting rid of some of her trash, and then we'll figure out if we need to move her body somewhere else. If we can even find it."

Carrie strained to hear what the men were saying, but they were all starting to fade away.

In fact, the entire room had started changing again.

The walls disappeared and the building seemed to dissolve right in front of her eyes. The ground beneath her feet transitioned from concrete to grass, and the ceiling above her turned into the pure darkness of night.

Carrie was shocked to now find herself standing outside in the middle of the woods. She still couldn't move, but it didn't matter anyway.

Where the hell can I go? I'm just going in circles here. It's probably better to just stand still and let fate take me where it will.

"You're right, dearie. It's all starting to make sense now, isn't it?"

And there, standing right next to Carrie, was Sandra Nunkes.

The woman was barefoot and wearing the peasant dress she'd been killed in. Her hair hung in ragged, frizzy strips. Sandra's face was rough and dirty, but it was her eyes that commanded the most attention.

They were wild orbs that bulged as if they wanted to escape their sockets but amazingly remained steadfast and fierce in their gaze. To Carrie they were like lasers of fire, threatening to burn a hole right through her.

Turning her head away so that she couldn't see Sandra's

awful face, Carrie willed herself to speak. "Why? Why us? I'm so sorry about what happened to you. But please let us go."

The crazed creature cackled. "Let ya go? Ha! Who let me go when I was surrounded by them people? Who let me live when all I did was keep to m'self? Eh?"

Carrie couldn't answer. She knew that Sandra was right. The woman may have been crazy, but she didn't deserve to die. The locals should have allowed the authorities to handle the matter.

"And why you? Oh, dearie. The answer is right in front of ya. Yer damned uncle Fred. Oh, wasn't he a sweet one? He never said nothing! Nothing! And he could've come clean. They all could've. But no one said a word. And now?"

Sandra raised her hands to the sky and laughed loudly. "Now, this is all mine! And you're just visitors here. Unless, like Anita and Roy … you decide to become my permanent guests."

It was all too much for Carrie, who threw her head back and screamed until the sound blocked out the terror and brought on total collapse.

Brett couldn't help himself.

Even though he knew he was supposed to be searching for the gate key or something sharp, the paperwork that was hidden within the different dusty boxes begged for his attention. Without noticing it, his fingers began sifting through reams and reams of yellowed invoices, statements, and financial information. As he tossed the papers to the floor and continued digging through the mountain of yellow-white sheets, his eyes widened when a stack appeared that was held together by a fragile rubber band.

A cover sheet had the words "Employees" written on it in marker.

When Brett turned the page, he read the name "Rick Duntman."

As the words sunk in, a distant memory came back to him. It wasn't a pleasant series of thoughts and had been hidden for so long that it took a moment for everything to connect.

Brett's memories only went back so far. Like most people, there was a singular point in his childhood when the reminders of pleasant and sometimes unpleasant things chose to stick within the corners of his mind. His earliest recollection was of attending a family get-together with his mother and father.

He vaguely remembered sitting in a high chair, wincing as his mother attempted to feed him some awful-tasting mush that was supposed to be a healthy oatmeal concoction. Even as a baby, Brett could recall how he had pursed his lips together, hoping to avoid any further food torture. But still, the spoon kept on coming and filling his tiny belly with the disgusting meal.

At some point during his feeding, another large body had approached and then taken his mother's place at the feeding spot. His mother had left the room for a moment—no doubt in search of a moment's peace after spending most of her time with a baby.

Brett remembered that the new feeder had started shoving morsel after morsel into his mouth. The food had come down quickly and confused him because it was beginning to make it hard to breathe.

Scared and confused, Brett had started waving his arms and kicking his feet until his mother had emitted a blood-curdling shriek and raced in, scooping him up and thumping him hard on the back until he'd vomited all the mush onto the floor.

Years later, the memory had re-emerged in Brett's mind during a breakfast that included some oatmeal, and he'd asked his mother about it.

"Mommy?"

"Yes, honey?"

"I remember something about oatmeal when I was really little. I've never really liked it, and I think it's because someone did something bad to me when I was eating it. Do you remember what happened?"

At the time, his mother had been wiping down the kitchen counter and suddenly hesitated, holding the dishrag in mid-swipe. She'd put her hands on the counter and looked out the window with a sad expression on her face.

"Mommy?" he'd asked again, wondering why she wasn't answering him.

His mother had turned around and left the dishrag on the counter, sitting down opposite him at the kitchen table. Even though the sun was streaming in through the window and casting warm rays throughout the breakfast nook, Brett had felt a chill run through him. He knew that his mother was about to tell him something serious.

"Honey, there are some people in this world who aren't quite right," she'd said. "Maybe they've lived through something awful, never got enough love from the people they care about, or just don't have all the light bulbs blinking at the same time. Do you understand what I'm trying to say?"

Brett had nodded, giving his mother a small smile and prompting her to continue.

"Well, one of Mommy's cousins suffered from some emotional problems. His name was Richard, but we all called him Rick for years. Anyway, Rick had a rough childhood and just never found his way. Now, what I'm about to tell you might be a little scary. Are you sure you're ready to hear it?"

Brett had been nine years old at the time and felt like he was big enough to hear the truth. And he was so curious anyway that he knew whatever his mother told him would be worth it.

"Your grandmother had a big Easter dinner when you were just about six months old. At the time, I was trying to help her get dinner prepared while also feeding you, because you liked to eat every three to four hours. You were such a hungry baby!" She'd laughed and given his hand a small squeeze. "Needless to say, I was kind of tired and when Rick said he'd help me feed you, I was more than happy to let him."

Her eyes had grown serious and the words that followed were spoken softly and carefully. "I left the room for about two minutes and when I came back, your cousin was putting oatmeal in your mouth. But somehow, he'd gotten distracted and was kind of looking away while he fed you. The problem was, he was stuffing your mouth with oatmeal and you were coughing—"

"You mean I was choking?" Brett had interrupted, his eyes wide.

"Um, yes. You were having a hard time swallowing all of it.

Anyway, it was a long time ago, and your cousin got sick not long after that with lung cancer. He passed away within the year. It's all very sad."

Brett had reached out and taken his mother's hand. He hated seeing her unhappy and wanted her to know that everything was all right. He was fine and his bad cousin Rick could never hurt him again.

That was the last time they had discussed his second cousin, but now, sitting in the dusty darkness, the memory was as clear as it had ever been. And the human resources paperwork in his hand listed Rick as someone who had worked at Sunken Park. In fact, according to the paperwork, Rick had been working at Sunken Park at the time of Sandra Nunkes's murder.

Did he know about it?

As Brett looked at the paper, there was no doubt in his mind that the Rick listed as an employee was his relative. For starters, there was a yellowed black and white photo attached by a small paperclip to the file that seemed very familiar, but everything else checked out, too; the age, the boy's home residence—it all pointed to Brett's second cousin.

As he flipped through the other pages, Brett was disappointed that none of the other names jumped out at him, but it was a good excuse to focus on the task at hand and find something to break open the padlock.

Need to focus. Stop messing around, he chided himself.

He pushed the box aside and lifted another one off a pile, dropping it to the ground with a large *thud*. The sound echoed through the small building and it was then that Brett realized how quiet everything had become. He'd been so immersed in his cousin's paperwork that he'd forgotten that Carrie was helping him search for a key or something to cut open the padlock.

"Carrie!" he called out. "You doing ok over there?"

There was no answer, which he found strange.

"Carrie! Are you ok?" he repeated.

When she didn't respond a second time, Brett began to get nervous. Hoisting himself up and dusting off his shorts, he looked around and called out a third time.

But the building was silent.

Damn it. I knew we should've stuck together. Now she's wandering around somewhere, and finding her is just going to take up more time.

Brett stepped into the hallway and felt all of the hairs on the back of his neck stand up.

Instead of standing in a hallway that ended at either an open doorway or the back wall, it now stretched out in both directions … seemingly infinite. At each end, the darkness beckoned with inky blackness spilling along the concrete floor and creeping frighteningly close to Brett's shoes.

Instinctively he stepped back, almost afraid to move in either direction.

"Brett!" Carrie voice suddenly shouted out. "Help me!"

He turned his head left and then right. It wasn't clear where the sound had come from, but somehow he knew that if he moved in the wrong direction, he'd never make it out alive.

"Where are you?" he called out.

At first, nothing responded to him. But then he felt a warm wind begin to blow through the hallway.

It was coming from what he deduced was the back of the building. A few dead leaves emerged from the gust, skimming along the floor; their shriveled brown bodies making a telltale scratching sound that reminded him of a spring long gone.

After a few more minutes of contemplating his fate, Brett decided to follow the direction of the wind. The other end of the hallway remained silent.

He swallowed hard and said a prayer.

As he walked slowly in the direction of the wind, he noticed that all of the rooms had disappeared and the walls were solid concrete. There weren't any cracks or weeds sprouting out along the surfaces either. They looked freshly painted and stern—like the walls of a prison for inmates who no longer deserved to see anything that would bring them a sense a comfort.

Brett reached out and touched one of the walls as he walked along slowly, shivering at the cool touch of the concrete. He immediately pulled his hand back and stuffed it into his shorts. Strangely, even though the hallway had initially seemed completely dark, it was now lit by a gloomy blue light that didn't seem to have an energy source.

The walls and floor *glowed*.

I can only imagine where this cursed place is going to take me, Brett thought. *But I can't just leave. I've gotta find Carrie.*

As he continued along the hallway, he noticed that it was no longer infinite. Now, he could see a sphere in the distance that glowed with the same bluish light and looked like an exit. The warm wind continued to blow through and at times, sent small pieces of dirt into the air, blinding Brett's eyes as he strained to look ahead.

The blue light grew more moderate and darkened as Brett approached the opening in the hallway. As he emerged through the space, it felt like he was exiting a cavern and had stepped outside once more.

A cursory look around revealed that he was once again standing in the middle of the Sunken Park woods. Tall pine trees surrounded him on all sides and in the distance, he could see the silver surface of the lake as the moonlight cast its reflection downward. He was now able to attribute the blue light he'd seen to the moon that hung low in the sky.

Yet, despite the familiar surroundings, Brett couldn't shake the feeling that somehow the world was different. There was a heavy, dreamlike quality to the air that made him feel as if he was a character in a movie and that the surroundings would change if he moved too quickly.

Still, there was no immediate danger, so he began walking through the woods. When he looked back, he could still see the spherical black opening of the strange hallway and made a mental note to get back there quickly.

I wonder if this is like one of those places where the portal to present day closes at a certain time. Sure wouldn't want to get lost in this dimension. Wherever this is.

As Brett walked through the woods, he instinctively stared at the ground below, hoping to see the familiar smooth path that could lead him in the right direction. This time, however, there was nothing but soft grass bracing his every step. The grass here felt smooth and dewy. It grew low to the ground and provided easy access as he made his way through the rows of trees.

Up above, the moon continued to guide his route, its center swollen and white. In the distance an owl hooted. Brett couldn't recall hearing any birds since they'd arrived and the more he thought about it, the weirder it seemed to him that the natural sounds of wildlife had been so muted during their visit.

But then this isn't a normal park, is it?

As Brett strained to see in the distance, his eyes were slowly able to make out a cabin. However, it wasn't the one he'd seen while walking along the trail.

This one was nestled within the foliage and was surrounded by weeds on all sides. It was old, broken down, and its windows were dark.

He considered whether or not to approach and then figured that something had obviously led him to this spot, so there was no choice but to continue forward.

It wasn't an easy approach. Bushes, branches, and weeds tore at him from all sides as Brett tried to maneuver around them. Spider webs stuck to his arms and hands as he pushed through. The area around the front of the cabin was barely clear of all the moss and greenery, and its door seemed to be hanging on by one rusty nail.

With a shaking hand, Brett put his hand on a dirty knob and pulled the door open. It swung easily, scraping the bottom of the floor as it opened. The sound was low and eerie and gave way to a dusty darkness within.

"Carrie?" he whispered. "Are you here?"

At the sound of his voice, the ground shook as if an earthquake had begun, and Brett nearly lost his footing. The entire cabin began to vibrate, and a yellow glow emerged from underneath the structure. It spread out from all sides and encapsulated the wooden house on each end, pouring into the windows and curling around the front door.

The light cast an unusual brightness on its surroundings and immediately the cabin began to change. The cobwebs and cracks disappeared and were replaced by newer wooden logs. The once-hazy windows cleared and the door straightened out miraculously, lifting up and properly connecting with the hinges.

The force caused Brett to lose his footing and he was now sitting on the floor in the cabin, hands outstretched for support, his eyes wide with disbelief. He wasn't sure what was happening, but whatever the glow was, it was changing the world around him and turning the broken-down cabin into a brand new structure that was full of life and … people?

To his shock, *people* began to appear within the cabin.

First he saw a group of middle-aged men and women materialize out of thin air. It was the group of people from the woods. There were also some faces that he recalled from the portraits that lined the wall in the park ranger's office. This group of people appeared one by one and were all standing with their backs against the far wall. They stood in a line and stared miserably down at their feet.

Then Roy and Anita appeared. They were both standing by the kitchen stove, staring at him as he watched from the doorway. Roy smiled strangely and slowly stuck his hand into a pot that was resting on the stovetop. Steam rose as his flesh burned and sizzled, but he didn't take his hand out or shriek in pain. He simply stared at Brett with an odd smile that never wavered.

Anita was still in the last stages of some horrible flesh-eating disease. Her body shook and dripped as flaps of skin tumbled from her small frame, but she wore the same strange grin. She stood next to Roy and placed a swollen, destroyed hand on her boyfriend's shoulder.

Brett wasn't sure what was going on, but he had a feeling that Anita and Roy were as dead as the people who he'd seen gathered in the park and who were now standing up against the wall. For started, all of the faces that were appearing were pale, with flat eyes and emotionless expressions. They were all slightly translucent … and behaving catatonic..

Swallowing hard, Brett tried to remember what he was hoping to accomplish. As he struggled with what to do next, all of the ghosts turned and faced the bedroom in the back. They didn't hesitate and moved as one entity, shifting their heads with the same robotic motion.

Brett stood warily, wiping the dust off his hands. His body

hurt from the stumble, and the last thing he felt like doing was staying in a cabin that seemed like a house of the dead. But once again, there was no choice. He knew that he had to move forward or face the possibility of losing Carrie forever.

He also wasn't sure how they were going to escape, but figured he'd retrace his steps back to the hallway entrance.

Easy peasy, right? Just need to make sure I don't end up like my cousin Rick. Or worse.

Taking a deep breath of the heavy air, Brett began to move forward. He carefully watched the ghosts as he walked through the cabin but they didn't turn around to face him. They all had their heads turned in the direction of the back bedroom.

Roy still had his hand in the boiling pot, and Anita continued to stand beside him, her bleeding hand on his shoulder.

"Roy. Anita. Are you guys ok?" Brett whispered, hoping to get a reaction, hanging on to a shred of hope that they were still alive.

But neither of them turned to look at him. They just stared forward …

Judging from their condition and odd behavior, Brett knew they were gone forever. There was nothing more he could do, so he refocused his attention on the bedroom door.

It was lit by a small lamp, and Brett recalled that a similar room in Cabin B had contained a single bed, a nightstand, and a basic dresser full of drawers. It was also where he'd seen Sandra and he knew that she was somehow responsible for all of this.

As he approached the bedroom, Carrie came into view. He could see that she was sitting on the side of the bed, her hands clasped in her lap. She had terror in her eyes, and he immediately recognized that she was not one of the ghosts he'd encountered in the main living room.

She was alive.

Swallowing hard, Brett tried to get Carrie's attention from the hallway but she was staring straight ahead and nervously wringing her hands. He wondered why she wasn't running out of room, but as he drew near, his question was answered.

"Come closer, Brett. We've been waiting for you."

Sandra's wretched voice carried towards him like a puff of

polluted smoke. He gagged at the scent of her breath, which smelled like an animal that had been dead for a long time. It permeated all of the breathable air, and for a moment Brett was afraid that he'd pass out.

Coughing, he put his hand against the wall and steadied himself. When he looked up again, Sandra was standing directly across from him, her back against the window that lined the cabin's western wall.

Her hair was flowing out in every direction and her white peasant dress also seemed to be flapping against an invisible wind. Her feet were several inches off the ground as she floated and leered at him.

"It's about time, dearie. I've been waiting here with Carrie. And all of my friends are here, too. Ain't it funny how people change their minds about you once it's too late?"

She cackled, and the awful sound filled the room.

Brett wanted to cover his ears to block out the cackling, but somehow he felt that if he moved it might indicate weakness so he stood his ground and watched her with defiant eyes.

"What do you want?" he asked with as much courage as he could muster.

"Me? Oh, dearie, I don't want anything no more. I have everything I could possibly want. I wanted the souls of those who wronged me, and I got 'em—forever. The ones who got away will come back to me eventually. Like yer sweet little cousin Ricky."

Brett stared at her, unsure of what to say.

"Yes, yer sweet little cousin who found pieces of my dress right beside a nasty looking patch of dirt. He decided to not say anything. Oh, no. He kept quiet just like the rest of 'em. I was murdered! And no one said one, little, itty-bitty word. And then, to make it even better? They named this here damned park after me. Changed the letters around a bit, but it's still mine."

Her rheumy eyes seemed to bore right into Brett's skull. Despite her haggard, zombie-like appearance, he was somehow was able to sense regret in the creature's tone.

This may be a deadly mistake, but I'm going to try it anyway, he thought.

Brett moved closer to the doorway. He caught Carrie's eyes and mentally tried to send her a message that everything would be ok. But he wasn't sure she could understand him as the terror in her irises flickered with the light of the fireplace. She didn't move or speak, and he wondered if perhaps she was frozen in place by a spell.

Sandra seemed surprised by his movement, but the creature recovered quickly and smiled at him as he approached.

"Well," she jeered, "seems you'd like to join us. Yer making this easy, boy."

"I want to talk to you," he said. "Are you willing to listen? Or do you think that everyone who approaches you is out to hurt you? I'm not one of those people. I promise you that."

And with all the strength he could muster, Brett strove to clear his heart and mind until he truly believed his own words. He had no grudge to satisfy, nothing to avenge. He was just a simple college kid who wanted to take his girlfriend and go home.

His words didn't seem to have an immediate impact on Sandra, but she didn't come closer to him and remained in her floating position, head cocked curiously.

Brett didn't wait for her to prompt him and began speaking quickly.

"What my cousin Rick did was wrong. Hell, what they all did was wrong—the locals who attacked and murdered you, the park ranger who led the charge, and the teenagers who turned their heads and did nothing to bring justice to such a horrible unnecessary crime."

"And they weren't their damned animals!" Sandra shrieked. "I'd found every one of those feral fuckers right here in the park. Many of 'em were barely alive. I'd skinned 'em and prepared 'em for medicine ... not food. And those photos? I took 'em cause I was lonely. Never had no kids of my own."

Even though he wasn't entirely sure what Sandra was talking about, Brett nodded and felt his courage begin to grow. "They shouldn't have harmed you. I know that and Carrie knows that. We also know how we're connected to you and what happened here. I understand your anger and your need for revenge. But please, don't take me and Carrie down to this dark place forever. We wouldn't have acted the same. Look deep into our souls and you'll see that we're different. We're good."

The creature seemed to hesitate and slowly lost the evil smile that had painted her face since he'd arrived at the cabin. Her body turned and she looked away for a minute, staring out of the window, her deadly breath fogging up the glass.

Brett looked over at Carrie and motioned for her to stand up. She blinked quickly and then slowly began to shift her legs as if the trance she'd been in was beginning to fade.

"They were so wrong," Sandra said, quietly. "I never wanted their kin or their pets. All I wanted was to be left alone. To be able to make my medicines and live my life in the trees and woods that had always protected me from bad things. From the things my daddy did to me. All I wanted was peace."

She turned her head back around quickly.

"But *they* took it from me. With their small minds and bad hearts. They took it from me and now they're gonna pay. Yer good friend Jack Blaze. He thought he knew it all. He thought he could kill me and get away with it."

She laughed again, but Brett was ready.

He quickly grabbed Carrie's hand and pulled her from the bed. She felt heavy, and it took nearly all of his strength to pull her out of a sitting position, but he wasn't taking any chances. He yanked her off the bed and threw her body out of the room, pushing her until she began running with him.

As they passed the ghosts in the living room, the creatures all turned their heads to face them. The movement was once again robotic and horrible, like a dance of the dead. Roy lifted his burnt and destroyed hand, and pointed to the door as if to say, *Get out. Get out now!*

Brett took Carrie's hand and they fled into the woods. He didn't pause to talk to her, just kept running through the trees and brush, nearly tripping on several large stones as they raced to safety. As he ran, he looked for the blackness of the hallway entrance.

At first he didn't see anything and just continued, racing past different trees and bushes.

Carrie was tiring and had begun to slow down, the weight of her body dragging his hand down.

"Don't slow down!" he called out to her. "We need to keep going. There's a way out—just follow me!"

She didn't answer and gave him a terrified look as her breathing continued in a heavy and frenzied pace.

He worried that she might not make it and was considering slowing down, when miraculously, the entrance to the mystical hallway came into view.

At first it appeared like a large black balloon hanging in midair, but as they drew closer it elongated and stretched out to the floor.

"Come on! We've got to get in there. Follow me."

Carrie seemed to find an additional reserve of energy and picked up the pace, running beside him as the sphere grew larger and larger. Finally, they felt the air change and the ground grow firmer as they passed through the entrance that led them back into the hallway. When their bodies were both inside gloomy darkness, the ground shifted again and another strange earthquake erupted around them.

Carrie stumbled and fell against Brett as the floor and the walls shifted back and forth, up and down, and then … stilled.

CHAPTER 15

"Is that it? Is it all over?"

Carrie's voice was soft, but it carried so much hope that it nearly broke Brett's heart. He wasn't sure if the ordeal *was* over. All he knew was that they were back inside the hallway, they were together, and there was no way he was going to leave her side again. No matter what.

He didn't answer, and led her back down the hallway in the other direction. It was no longer infinite and he could clearly see the entrance to the structure, with the yellow hazard tape blowing along the ground in front of the opening. As they walked through it, he barely looked in either direction. It didn't really matter anymore.

They simply needed to get out.

Whatever it took.

"Brett, we can't leave. We don't have the key to the gates, and we don't have anything to pry them open. How are we going to get the car out? We can't drive through it."

He turned to face her. "We can't waste another minute here looking for something to help us. It's too dangerous. Are you ok?"

She gave him a small smile. "Yeah, if you mean am I ok even though a ghost hag captured me and kept me in her cabin? Yeah, I'm doing fine. Thanks for asking."

Brett chuckled. She was right. It was a ridiculous question given the circumstances. He decided it would be better to ask questions later and just focus on getting out.

Once they stepped outside the building, he took a deep breath. It felt like a huge weight had been lifted off of his shoulders. Thankfully his car was still parked beside the gates and perhaps it was possible to drive through them. It would be risky and they might get injured, but he didn't see any other way out.

"Come on, let's get in the car," he said, tugging on her hand to get her to hurry up.

But Carrie wasn't moving.

"Come on, what's the problem?" he asked and turned around. When he saw what she was staring at, he also stopped moving.

The doorway to the building had begun to glow again with a dull blue haze, and this time—there was no moon to attribute it to. It was simply generating from inside the structure.

As he stood and looked in the direction of the light, he began to make out several figures emerging. They weren't walking along the ground and appeared to be floating in unison. He squinted and saw that Anita and Roy were among the group of ghosts, and at the center Sandra Nunkes was floating in mid-air, her gaze focused steadily on them.

Carrie screamed in fright, and Brett nearly urinated in his pants. Somewhere deep in his mind, a small voice was screaming at him to *run!*

Run!

The voice was quiet at first and then grew louder and louder, shaking him out of his terrified state.

"Carrie, we've got to get out of here! Come on!" he shouted as he pulled her backwards and pushed her in the direction of his car. He fumbled around in his shorts pocket and nearly cried out in relief when his fingers curled around the smooth metal of his car keys.

He quickly pulled them out and, with shaking hands, disengaged the alarm and unlocked the doors.

Carrie got into the passenger's seat and he jumped into the car and quickly shoved the key into the ignition. As he looked up, he could now see that the ghosts had come out of the building and were steadily moving toward them.

"Shit. Let's go, let's go!" he urged the vehicle as he put the car into reverse and backed up as quickly as he could. The rear tires were now only a few feet away from the approaching ghosts, and he didn't even want to think about what would happen if they somehow were able to get inside the car with them.

"Hang on! Here we go!" he shouted.

He put his foot on the pedal and pushed it to the ground, using as much gas as possible to get through the gate.

The car accelerated quickly, but as the gate arms grew closer, Brett realized that Carrie was not wearing her seatbelt. He turned to her and shouted, "Put on your seatbelt! Put on your—"

And then the car crashed into the arms of the gate at nearly fifty miles per hour.

A huge explosion erupted in front of Brett's eyes as the glass from the windshield shattered into pieces. In his peripheral vision, he though he saw Carrie fly out of her seat and into Sandra's ghostly arms.

Then his head hit the airbag and all went black.

CHAPTER 16

Pain was everywhere.

It started in his toes, then spread to his arms and raced across his chest in zigzagging spears of fire. But his eyes felt the worst. They seemed to be stinging from the inside out.

This is it. I'm dying. This must be what death feels like.

Brett opened his eyes and could only see black pebbles. He turned his head and came in contact with more sharp, unforgiving stones.

"Ouch," he murmured as he tried to lift himself up. At first he was a bit hazy as to how he'd ended up on the ground. But when he saw his car in the distance, it became clear. He'd driven into the gates trying to escape Sunken Park.

But how did I end up here?

Brett was no longer inside the park. He was staring at his damaged car, which was still on the other side of the gates.

But he was not on the same side. He was lying on the gravel road that was located in the large clearing that separated the trees from the gates leading to the park.

His head was pounding and hurt in a million places, but somehow Brett managed to stand up. When he put his hand to his forehead, he felt wetness.

Great. I'm bleeding. Wait—where the hell is Carrie?

"Carrie!" he called out.

The wind howled through the trees in the distance as a warm wind swept through the branches. But Carrie didn't answer him.

But I can't be alone. She's gotta be somewhere. I've gotta find her.

Brett looked at his car. It was smashed up against the gate

arms, the front end a total disaster. The tires were flat and a low whooshing noise carried toward his ears, which indicated that something was either leaking or expelling fumes.

He wasn't sure how he'd survived the impact and, frankly, why he'd tried to break the gates open in the first place. It was a dumb move, but one obviously borne out of desperation.

As he walked toward the gate, he strained to see if Carrie was in the car. A lump formed in his throat as he neared the wreckage.

If she's dead, I'll never forgive myself.

When the car fully came into view, he could clearly see how much damage had been done. The front of the vehicle was smashed in, with different fluids leaking everywhere. The windshield was so damaged that it was hard to see if Carrie was still inside, but somehow the glass had held together, so it was impossible for someone to have been ejected from the car.

Unless …

Brett wondered if the ghosts had intervened somehow. Perhaps Sandra had taken pity on them and allowed them to escape.

Or only allowed me to escape.

He considered hopping over the gate arms and was about to swing his legs over the side when a shimmering light appeared in the distance. His entire body tensed as he instinctively prepared for another encounter with an entity that was trapped within the confines of the haunted woods.

The image began to take shape and, to his surprise, melded into a woman. When the figure entirely transformed, it became a familiar one, and as the ghost approached, Brett felt tears begin to form in the corners of his eyes as the sadness of what could have been began to descend upon him.

"You must leave," it said.

"I can't, Carrie. I can't leave you here. You don't deserve to die this way. Please don't leave me like this."

The Carrie-ghost was pale and shimmering, but did not appear to be in any pain or discontent. She smiled as she floated closer to him and came close enough for him to see tiny pinpricks of light radiating off of the periphery of her skin.

"Darling Brett. Please don't worry about me. I'm fine here. We'll all be fine here. Sandy can't hurt me now. And she doesn't want to. She just needs me to help her watch over these woods. This is where I belong. But she let you go. She saved you."

"Carrie, you don't know what you're saying. Please come with me. Please." Brett began to lift his leg in preparation to climb over the gates.

The ghost grew serious and the light that glowed around her darkened to a deeper shade of violet. Her eyes blazed and she spoke louder; her voice so stern that it stopped Brett in his tracks.

"You cannot pass over. Don't come back here, Brett. Don't ever come back. Turn around and walk away. And don't ever tell anyone of this place. We'll handle it so that our deaths are accounted for. You must leave this mountain and never return. Please. If you come back, I cannot guarantee your safety. Sandy allowed you to leave, but she may not be so forgiving the next time. She will not harm me. Please go."

Brett wanted to say something else to keep Carrie from leaving him, but could tell that she was already starting to fade. She cocked her head as if waiting for a response, and then waved slowly like a beauty pageant queen and turned. Her figure floated off into the distance and then disappeared in a warm gust of wind, leaving Brett alone once more in the middle of the clearing.

He wasn't sure what to do next, so he sat on the ground and cried tears of sorrow and regret. Eventually his mind shut down completely and he fell into a dreamless black sleep.

As is customary for the world, the sun appeared within the next hour and promised a new dawn.

The purple and orange hues of the warm rays stretched out across the horizon, creating a landscape of god-like serenity and brought with them the warmth of another day.

Brett's eyelids felt the heat of the approaching morning, and he slowly opened them. His vision was blurred at first, with grains of dust and dirt caking his eyelashes together. As he rubbed his face and gingerly sat up, he found himself face to face with his car.

It was no longer on the other side of a gate that led to the entranceway of a park, but instead was parked a few yards away on the grass.

It appeared to be in perfect condition.

He shook his head, expecting to wake up from a nightmare that included Carrie, Roy, and Anita.

It was all a nightmare, wasn't it? They're all ok, right? But if it was a dream, then what am I doing out here in the middle of nowhere, sleeping on the grass in front of my car?

Brett stood up and walked over to his vehicle. The door on the driver's side was unlocked, and the keys were still in the ignition. He left the door open and did a full inspection, walking around the car and checking under the hood. Everything appeared fine to him.

But everything wasn't fine.

"Tough night, eh?"

Brett didn't even turn around. The sound of Jack Blaze's voice was not entirely a surprise, but it confirmed that the nightmare had been real and his friends were lost to him forever.

"Yep. Wasn't a great one. What're you doing here? Are you trying to gloat?"

"Turn around, son. We need to talk."

He turned his head and once again stared into the weathered face of a man he now knew was long gone. The park ranger was dead and just another member of the cursed mountain park.

But Jack didn't seem threatening now in the early light of morning. The ranger's countenance turned downward in a saddened, thoughtful gaze, and it occurred to Brett that the poor soul was trapped and couldn't really hurt him.

"Ok, I'm listening."

Jack sighed and looked back in the direction of the park. "I'm sure sorry you and your friends came here. Most folks don't stumble across this way very often. But it looks like y'all didn't have much of a choice. You're connected to us in one way or the other. By now you probably know that your cousin Rick was one of the kids we had working here during those dark times."

Brett nodded.

"Well, he's not here with us. Somehow he lived his life and was able to die far away from these woods. And Sandy, well, she must've seen something in you to let you go like that. But don't take it for granted. Do yourself a favor and get in your car and drive away. When you get home, you'll discover that none of your friends ever got in your car or went on a trip with you. They've all died in their own way."

The park ranger began to walk back in the direction of the woods and turned to face Brett one last time.

"You're lucky, son. I think Sandy saw what Rick tried to do to you when you were a youngster. He tried to hurt you just like he did her. And because of that she felt like you deserved to live." The ghost shook his head as if trying to fully grasp that fact and then chuckled, tipped his hat, and disappeared into the woods.

CHAPTER 17

Brett gripped the wheel tightly as he maneuvered along the small road that led back to the main stretch of highway. His mind raced in a million directions and when he looked at his cell phone, he was surprised to see that the signal had returned and numerous emails had begun appearing on the translucent face.

One of them was from his friend Gary that had the title of "So sorry to hear about Roy."

He swallowed hard and thought about what Jack had said. All of his friends were dead. Carrie was dead. He was all alone in the knowledge of the horrific night they had endured and would forever carry the memory.

As he watched the road intently, Brett was aware that there were figures in the distance that were barely tickling his peripheral vision. His curiosity gnawed at him and he itched to look at them, but he knew that one slip and his car would veer off track.

The trees surrounded his vehicle on all sides as he slowly worked his way to the highway and when the bright dusty opening appeared in the distance, he let out a sigh of relief. The smooth feel of the road under his tires was a welcoming sensation, and it was only when he was a good mile away from the turn off that he allowed himself to breathe easy.

Brett drove for nearly twenty minutes in silence and then finally pulled off at a gas station that doubled as a convenience store. He parked the car and picked up his phone, scrolling through the emails. His friend Eric had emailed him an hour prior and sent a rambling message about the awful fate that had taken their colleagues. Brett's eyes misted over as he read the email:

"Hey man, hope you're doing ok. We can't believe what's happened. It's totally the craziest and most horrible thing ever. The whole school's talking about it. Losing three students in one day. Hell, it doesn't seem real.

"Jerome gave Roy's mom a call, and she's not doing too good. We don't understand how he could have drowned. He was such a good swimmer, but they say the current was real strong when he was in the river by their house. And Anita wasn't a good swimmer. She never had a chance after jumping in after him. It's really sad how bad she ended up. One of her friends told me that her body got all cut up from the rocks, and she was so injured that it was hard to identify her.

"And how about that Carrie girl? I know you had a serious crush on her. So sorry. Can't believe what happened to her. They say her parents always lit fires in their house with no problem. What are the chances that there was a gas leak the night she decided to sleep downstairs? At least she died quickly, but fuck! She was so young.

"Well, anyway, I hope you're ok. Some of the guys said you left here in the morning looking for some 'alone time' and that you took off for the mountains. Whatever, dude. Come back so we can grab a beer and talk about things. There's some good college football games on, and we can lean on each other. Roy would've wanted that.

"Come back and let's hang. Give me a call when you get this."

Brett smiled through his tears. Ranger Jack Blaze was right. Life did go on, and no one was the wiser. Somehow whatever had taken place in Sunken Park had been replaced by natural, tragic occurrences. But Brett wondered if everything had been wiped away and history had somehow been reset.

Will Carrie remember me? Or what we shared during those fateful hours? How can I be sure?

Just then, he looked out across the street and for a split

second he saw his three friends standing on the other side. Roy and Anita were holding hands and smiling at him. Carrie stood next to them and smiled, then cocked her head as if to say, "Hey, cheer up. We're ok."

Brett considered getting out of the car, but just as he put his hand out to open the door, the images began to shimmer and then disappeared.

Looking over his shoulder for oncoming traffic, Brett backed out of the parking spot and onto the highway. As he drove, he wept and made a quick decision to call his mother and father more often. In the background, a song was playing on the radio that reminded him of a beautiful blonde girl he'd once known.

1989   Pine Mountain, Georgia

The door to the office swung shut behind them as the teenagers left the park ranger's building.

They were shaken by what they'd just heard and knew that they'd been told to do something bad. The air around them tasted sour and sharp. No one spoke for a few minutes.

Finally, the redheaded girl sighed loudly and ran two slender fingers through her long hair. "This is wrong, you guys. We can't not say anything. You know that something happened to that woman. We've all checked her cabin and it's empty. She didn't just disappear into thin air. And what about you, Rick? You saw something in the dirt, didn't you? Why didn't you say anything?"

"Tina, be quiet. We don't know what we saw," muttered Dewayne Johnson, a handsome African American teenager with serious eyes. "You heard what Ranger Blaze said. We need to chill out about all of this."

Another teen, this one shyer than the rest, looked over at the group and quietly disagreed. "I don't think I can go back to work just yet. I wanna see it again. Don't you?" he asked.

The others in the group looked at each other questioningly. They'd been told to steer clear of the area, but there were no adults around. All of the park rangers and full-time staffers had gone inside and were having a private "meeting" that didn't include the part-timers.

Tina nodded her head slowly. "Yeah. I wanna know that we're not all losing our minds. Let's just go back one more time, and then we'll never go there again."

The only one who seemed a bit hesitant was Dewayne. He'd

come across the mud pits before and knew that after it rained a person could end up sinking deep within the murky depths of the filth. It wasn't a pleasant thought, and he knew that the rains had only ended in the morning hours so everything was still dewy and moist.

"I'm not sure," he said, almost to himself. "Is it really worth it? Let's just get back to work."

"No," Tina argued stubbornly. "We need to see it. Just one more time. If you want to stay here, that's fine, but I'm going."

The teens took a look behind them at the closed door and quickly set off together into the woods. As they walked along the familiar foliage, they kept their chatter to a minimum. It was clear that they were taking a risk. Their supervisor had asked them to steer clear of the mud pits that boarded the park perimeter, but their young minds burned with curiosity. They just *had* to see if there was someone or something in the strange muck near Sandra's home.

As they passed one of the cabins, Tina saw the Martin family in the distance. They appeared to be boxing up their belongings. She's heard a rumor that the county had decided to move the residents to another location and eventually open up more land to the park so that it could cater to additional overnight guests.

But she felt bad for the families that had made their home here, deep within this portion of the Pine Mountain woods. For the most part they were clean and kept to themselves. Sure they had some annoying kids and sometimes left soda cans or cigarette butts in the grass, but they were good people and Tina felt that it was unfair to relocate people from one place to another just because they didn't have any money. She waved at one woman who'd always been nice to her, but didn't receive a warm greeting in return. The woman just looked at her with a serious face and closed the door.

The park had a strange, irregular border than ran parallel to the smattering of cabins and then opened out into a part of the mountain that began a sharp incline. That area of Pine Mountain was difficult to navigate, with cliffs jutting out in different spots—the drop below deep and deadly.

The group was careful to keep their distance and as they

neared the clearing where the ground tended to become muddy and even dangerous, Rick slowed down considerably. He was rethinking his decision. After all, he'd been totally creeped out when he'd come into contact with the strange cloth that had been sticking out of the dirt.

And there had been *hair* attached to it.

At the time he'd discovered the artifact, he'd been horrified, but also mesmerized. Awkward and painfully shy all of his life, Rick yearned to be at the center of something really important. Seeing the strange object in the middle of the park had made his heart pound and also excited him.

But now, everyone would see it, and he wasn't sure he liked that idea.

"Come on, Rick!" Tina shouted back at him. "You're moving too slow!"

As the cluster of trees began to spread out, the group moved in closer and crowded around a small clearing that was devoid of bushes and shrubs. The ground was rough, and there were dark spots along the dirt, some quite large, indicating moist soil below.

Dewayne shuddered. He knew what that meant. They were close to the area where many animals sank to their deaths. It was a dark, strange place, and he felt as if they were being watched.

"Let's get this over with."

Tina walked to the blackened patch in the middle and squatted in front of it. At first, she didn't see anything strange. The dirt looked rough, with rocks seeming to float on the surface of jutting crags that were flecked with green moss.

"Nasty," she muttered. "So where is it, Rick? I don't see anything weird."

"You're not looking in the right spot. I think it was kinda off to the side."

Tina knelt closer to the ground and continued to scour the landscape. Her eyes darted back and forth until she noticed a small piece of white material. It was muddy and inconspicuous as it stuck to a partially submerged stone.

"Aha! I see it," she whispered excitedly.

As Tina put out her hand to touch it, Dewayne snapped, "Don't touch the fucking thing! You don't know what it is!"

The sound of his voice caught the redhead off guard and she stumbled, falling face-first into the muck. She screeched and pulled herself out of the dirt, now covered from head to toe in wet, shiny filth.

"Fuck!" she screamed. "You scared me. And now—"

Suddenly, one of the members of the group, a small Hispanic girl who was normally timid and a typical wallflower, let out a small moan. Her face had turned pale and she was staring at something not far from where Tina now sat.

Dewayne looked in the direction of her terrified gaze and he saw it, too.

In fact, they all saw it, and would never forget that day for the rest of their lives. The vision would forever haunt them as they tried to go on with their business and forget about the horror that lived in the park. They'd grow older and some would have their own children, but they'd all struggle with the knowledge that something in the world was not quite right. Some of them would wake up in the middle of the night screaming and praying that the memory would fade away.

But it never would.

Because in the darkened clearing, a few feet away from Tina's dirtied knees, a small white hand was emerging from the muck. Its nails were torn and scraggly with dirt heavily embedded under them.

The teenagers collectively gasped as the hand rose from the mud—all the way to the top of its wrist—and then turned, pointing an accusing finger at all of them.

"Holy fucking shit," Dewayne whispered, and they ran from the clearing, never looking back.

The next day, the group returned to the park and promptly quit—in unison. It was the first time in park history that such a large group of part-timers had resigned, and to the adults who remained in the small facility building harboring deadly secrets, it was a sign of bad things to come.

And bad things were definitely coming to Sunken Park in Pine Mountain, Georgia.

ABOUT THE AUTHOR

Sara Brooke is an Amazon bestselling author of horror, paranormal romance, and suspense fiction.

A lifelong avid reader of all things scary, Sara's childhood dream was to write books that make readers sleep with their lights on. She hopes that isn't too troubling for the thousands of readers worldwide who have purchased her books.

Sara has been published alongside horror legends Clive Barker and John Carpenter. She has written nine novels and numerous short stories.

Sara resides in beautiful South Florida. She can be reached via her website at www.sarabrooke.com. Sara welcomes feedback and questions from readers.

Curious about other Crossroad Press books?
Stop by our site:
http://store.crossroadpress.com
We offer quality writing
in digital, audio, and print formats.

Enter the code FIRSTBOOK
to get 20% off your first order from our store!
Stop by today!

www.ingramcontent.com/pod-product-compliance
Lightning Source LLC
Chambersburg PA
CBHW061247170626
46809CB00007B/2874